Cassie turned to him, worried. "What if we don't win? This contest means everything to me."

John nodded. "I get that. It means a lot to me, too. But I can't think that way about losing and neither should you. I have to focus on being the best at what I do and proving to them all that I'm just as good as they are."

She rested her hand on his. "You are good. Better than good. You blow me away with some of your ideas. It's been my privilege to work with you."

He reached out and touched her cheek. "The privilege is all mine, Cass."

She dropped her gaze from his, aware of how vulnerable she'd made herself to him. Wondering if he would accept her words, accept her. And why did it matter so much if he did?

Dear Reader,

Did something ever happen to you that changed the path you'd been following? Maybe it was a job loss or the death of a parent. Maybe it was the breakup of a relationship that you thought would never end. Whatever it was, it changed your life from one you expected to something you didn't recognize.

If you've read my books before, you know that divorce and cancer were two things that changed the path I'd been traveling. They made me stop in my tracks and start asking the big questions. What followed were times of amazing personal growth and change, but it wasn't easy to start imagining a different future.

I don't know about you, but I love reading stories about people getting a second chance. About those who take their losses and turn their lives into something beautiful. In this story, Cassie had planned to take over her father's construction company, and John thought he'd keep designing award-winning cars. But they are about to find out that sometimes the best plan is to embrace the unknown.

If you're going through one of those times of losses and searching for a new path, don't give up. Just hold on because a better day is coming.

Syndi

HEARTWARMING

Their Forever Home

——

Syndi Powell

H HARLEQUIN® HEARTWARMING™

Recycling programs
for this product may
not exist in your area.

ISBN-13: 978-1-335-51084-6

Their Forever Home

Copyright © 2019 by Cynthia Powell

Printed in U.S.A.

Syndi Powell started writing stories when she was young and has made it a lifelong pursuit. She's been reading Harlequin romance novels since she was in her teens and is thrilled to be on the Harlequin team. She loves to connect with readers on Twitter, @syndipowell, or on her Facebook author page, Facebook.com/syndipowellauthor.

Books by Syndi Powell

Harlequin Heartwarming

Visit the Author Profile page
at Harlequin.com for more titles.

This book is dedicated to all the dogs I've loved before: Midnight, Kohlby, Furio, Phoebe, Gracie Lou, Shiloh, Cody, Rocky, Ladybird, Reno, Evie, Pinot, Bella, Katie and Ceasar. And in memory of my beloved kitty, Diva. You've all made my life better.

And thank you to my parents, Russ and Pattie D'Hondt, who helped inspire this new book series by helping me brainstorm ideas for the plot. Thank you also for watching home renovation shows with me for research.
I love you both.

CHAPTER ONE

THE BALLROOM AT the Whittier Hotel in downtown Detroit glittered under the dozen chandeliers that hung from the high ceiling. Cassie Lowman felt a crick in her neck start to form as she stared at the opulent murals decorating the ceiling above her head. While it wasn't her favorite aesthetic, she could appreciate the artistry. Too ornate and fussy for her—she would rather have something be beautiful in its simplicity.

A tuxedoed waiter passed by with a tray of half-filled champagne flutes. She snagged one before returning her gaze to the ceiling. She lifted her glass for a brief salute and then started to scan the room for familiar faces.

In truth, most of the faces were known to her as well as their names. These were her father's former competitors—building contractors who had rejoiced when he'd failed and patted themselves on their backs while they swooped in and stole his clientele. She tasted the bitterness and anger at the back of her throat, so she tipped the champagne flute and drank the bubbly liquid before leaving the empty glass on a nearby table. Maybe it was better for her to look for new friends.

Speaking of friends, the Buttucci brothers, Tiny and Biggie, waved at her from the other side of the ballroom. She started to wobble in her shoes as she walked toward them. Blast her mother for insisting she wear high heels to this kickoff event. She wasn't a heels kind of woman. Nor a fancy dress type, either, she thought, as she tugged at the neckline. It wouldn't be so bad if she had something to flaunt, but she knew her limitations.

Biggie held a beer in his hands, and Cassie eyed it with envy. She approached the brothers, who were like family to her, especially now that she hoped to be helming the business, rather than her dad. "I'm glad you two could come. I don't know if I could face this alone, chosen or not."

Tiny looked behind her. "Your mother's not here?"

"Mother decided that if she came with me that it would mean she approved of this venture." Cassie shook her head. "And we all know where she stands on that."

Tiny put his hand on her shoulder. "She'll get over it in time."

"Yesterday, her last words on the phone to me were, and I quote, 'Forget the company already. It's an anchor dragging you down.' End quote." Not that the company had many assets left after her father had taken most of them when he disappeared, and the rest had been sold to pay off debts. She'd had to tell employees who had been with her father for decades that they should seek employment elsewhere. Even her sister who had been the construction office's receptionist had found a new job within weeks of his disappearance. The only two who had refused to leave her stood with her now. Cassie tugged again at the dress she'd borrowed from her older sister. "She doesn't get it. I want to win the quarter of a million prize money so that I can start the business over and hire everyone back."

Biggie grunted and sipped his beer while Tiny patted her shoulder again. "It will all work out. It always does."

She wished she had his confidence. Her father's building company seemed to be just another thing that stood between her and her mother. Growing up, Cassie had heard about how ladies didn't come home covered in sawdust or with calloused hands. Ladies wore dresses, not plaid shirts and jeans. Her older sister, Andromeda, had filled the bill according to her mother's requirements. Couldn't her mother be happy that she had one perfect daughter?

But Lowman Construction meant something to Cassie, even if her mother had turned her back on it. Not only had it been her means of income, it was her lifeblood. She'd put years of her life into it at her father's side, and she hoped to continue without him. She wanted to bring it back to what it had once been. She had to.

Cassie glanced again at Biggie's beer. "Where can I get one of those?"

He pointed to a long wood-and-brass bar where several people milled, and she walked toward it. People murmured as she passed them, but she chose to hold her head high and ignore the comments. She paused a moment when she tottered again and the heel on one shoe threatened to bend and snap, but she slowed her gait and joined the line of those waiting for a drink.

She heard a scratchy voice talking ahead of her and recognized the gravelly tones of Bill Swenson, one of her father's chief rivals. "I don't understand why some people can't let go of failure and get on with their lives. Did you see her name on the list? Does she have to waste her time and ours by entering this contest?"

A man next to him sneered. "Bill, you know why she entered. To redeem her father's name."

Cassie swallowed again at the bitter taste in her mouth. They could only be talking about her. She thought about leaving the line without getting her beer, but the temptation to eavesdrop was too great.

Bill laughed. "Redeem? She'd have to do a lot more than win some contest to do that. How about paying back the people he stole from? You ask me, she's cut from the same cloth as her old man." He spotted her. Giving her a sardonic grin, he winked. "I'll be keeping my eye on you."

Tears threatened to choke her, but she wasn't going to let anyone, especially Bill, see how the words affected her. They didn't know anything about her. Didn't know that she had been just as shocked by the allegations of embezzlement against her father. As heads turned to look at her, she stood straighter, refusing to ignore their stares. "You can watch me all you want as I win this thing, Bill. The Belvedere Foundation won't accept substandard materials and shoddy work. Isn't that why you lost the Stamper contract?"

Bill bristled and took a step toward her, but someone pulled him back and ordered him a drink. Most of the others who had listened to the conversation turned away from her and joined him. Cassie put a hand on her chest and felt her heart beating with speed. She wouldn't run now. She had to prove to them all that she was as good as them, if not better. She could rebuild beautiful houses as well as her own life.

WITH A GLASS of whiskey in his hand, John Robison leaned on the bar and looked at the woman whose cheeks had colored at the blustering contractor's words. He could admire someone who wouldn't back down from a confrontation with a bully. Took a lot of guts to keep your head high when others were trying to tear you down. The woman made her way up to the front of the bar and ordered a beer. Her dark brown eyes reminded him of the color of bourbon. "You have something to say, too?"

He shook his head and looked her over. She was petite, but he sensed that there was a lot of power in that compact frame. "No, ma'am."

"Ma'am." She rolled her eyes. "So polite."

"The way my mama raised me."

She eyed him with a gleam of speculation. "I know most of the people here, but I don't think we've met before." She held out her hand. "Cassie Lowman."

"John Robison." He took her hand into his and felt the calluses on them. "You're a contractor?"

She gave a short nod and accepted the tall glass of beer the bartender handed her. "Rough hands tend to give away my profession. Your smooth hands tell me you're a designer."

"Guilty. I usually hold pencils instead of hammers and saws. This will be my first time designing a house, though."

"First time? And you entered a contest like this without any experience?"

"I have plenty of design experience, and I've won contests like this in the past. They just happened to be designs for cars." Five awards to be exact, but who was counting? He didn't need to have experience with houses to win this thing. His art training could be translated into many different avenues, but seeing the contest announced in the newspaper had seemed to be a sign of which one to follow.

"Designing a house that has both function and beauty is a completely different animal than a vehicle designed for speed. I'm afraid you're in over your head here, Mr. Robison."

"Well, the contest committee disagrees

with you, or I wouldn't have made it this far."

She narrowed her eyes at him. "No offense, Mr. Robison, but I hope that we're not paired together. I need an experienced designer. That is, if you make it into the top five."

If? He had every intention to not only make it into the top five teams, but to win the entire contest. And he'd be more than happy to make her eat her words. "With that attitude, Ms. Lowman, the feeling is mutual. I need a contractor who has an open mind rather than one who has already decided what is right."

She took her beer and turned away, her legs teetering on heels that added a couple of inches to her height, but she had only met him at chest level. If he wasn't so concerned about this contest, he might follow her and strike up another conversation. See if he could find more to admire about her. But he wasn't here to make friends. He needed to prove that he had the ideas and skills to win this thing.

A gentleman in a bow tie and suit tapped on a microphone situated on a platform at one end of the ballroom. Finally. *Let's get this party going.*

"Ladies and gentlemen, members of the press, my name is Christopher Belvedere, and I'm pleased to announce the kickoff for the Belvedere Foundation's premier Take Back the Neighborhood contest."

The din of conversation dropped to a lull as people started to gather closer to the platform. John joined them and looked around at his competitors.

"Since 1923 when the first Thomas Belvedere opened a construction company in Detroit, the family has been devoted to improving the city that built us. We built neighborhoods—homes, schools and the St. Anne hospital. When the third Thomas Belvedere created special software, not only did it revolutionize the design of architecture, its multi-million dollar success provided the funds to create the Belvedere Foundation. Since 1971 through additional fundraising, the foundation has financed several thousand low-interest mortgages to families who might not have otherwise had the opportunity to purchase their own home.

"As you know, the foundation recently

bought five abandoned houses from the city of Detroit that were set for demolition. Our goal has always been to bring back the city of Detroit, one house at a time. It is our hope that the selected contractors and designers will bring their expertise into turning these spaces into incredible homes. The winning team will win a quarter of a million dollars, a national and regional magazine spread for their winning design, and be featured in a television special on the Home Design Network. The other teams will win a smaller monetary prize and regional recognition in magazine and newspaper articles." The gentleman stopped and glanced around the ballroom. "We had more than a hundred applicants for the ten slots. Through interviews and portfolio presentations, we winnowed the pool to the top ten contractors and top ten designers, all of whom are present this evening. After much deliberation to finalize the five teams, it is my pleasure to announce who will be competing over the next three months. Remember all work is to be completed twelve weeks from today!"

The knot in John's belly tightened. He

knew that his portfolio had been strong enough to get him into the top ten designers. He hadn't graduated at the top of his class in art school for nothing. Unfortunately, he didn't interview very well, and he feared that would keep him from being chosen. He closed his eyes and said a silent prayer. He'd put everything he had into this contest. He needed this affirmation of his abilities. Being laid off due to budget cuts and downsizing had shaken his confidence.

Shaking off his doubts, he listened as the first two teams were announced. The blustery bully made snide comments after each name, and John walked away from his group to distance himself. He didn't need that kind of negativity to feed into his own fears. He glanced around the room and saw Cassie standing between two beefy men who looked like they could be her bodyguards. She bit her lip as the third team was announced.

He sipped his whiskey and almost choked when he heard his name. Someone boomed out, "Who in the world is that?"

John set his glass down and started to walk toward the platform, where the other teams waited. Mr. Belvedere continued, "And paired with Mr. Robison is Cassandra Lowman of Lowman Construction."

He caught Cassie's wide-eyed stare. So they were going to be thrown together after all. Well, it could be worse. He might have been paired with the bully.

STILL IN SHOCK at hearing her name, Cassie felt Biggie pat her on the shoulder and Tiny nudge her toward the platform. She'd done it. She'd made it into the top five contractors. Until this moment, she hadn't realized how uncertain she'd been of succeeding in this.

She closed her mouth and took careful steps toward the stage. The applause that followed after her name had been read out was softer than that for her competitors, and she knew it was because of her father, but it had stung all the same. Would there be a day when it wouldn't hurt?

John stood on the stage and watched her as she approached the three steps. She took the first step, teetered because of the heels and then felt his hands on her elbow and waist as he helped her. She whispered her thanks and joined the other teams as the last two names were announced.

"Let's hear it for our top five teams!" Mr. Belvedere turned with a flourish of his hands, and she heard the applause.

She tried to smile as photographers took their pictures and reporters yelled out questions. She hoped that she at least appeared composed and confident, because she felt anything but those things on the inside. What had she done? Did she really think she could pull this off? Maybe her mother was right? Maybe she should have agreed to let go, sell the company and start over in a different career. But something deep down had told her that she could do this. She clung to that hopeful ember and straightened her spine.

"Ms. Lowman, have you heard from your father? Does he know you entered the contest?"

"Do you know where your father is hiding?"

"Have you given any evidence to the police?"

The smile on her face threatened to fade, but she hung on to it. She wouldn't let their questions take away from her moment. Because this was about her, not her father. This was about her talents and abilities. Her time to shine, not to hide in shame.

John leaned down and whispered into her ear, "Just keep smiling."

She gave a short nod and hoped that this would be over soon. She could see the brothers clapping, Tiny beaming while Biggie wiped at his tears with a faded red bandanna.

Finally, the announcer gathered the five teams in a lopsided circle and handed them all manila envelopes. "Inside the packet, you'll find the address of the house you'll be working on along with the keys. Your budget is included along with a list of pre-approved subcontractors." He turned to Cassie. "I've already approved the Buttucci brothers' application to work on your team."

"Thank you. I'm pleased to know that," she replied.

"We will have an in-depth meeting Monday morning at nine at the foundation's office to go over everything that is required of you. In the meantime, go out and mingle. Talk to the press. Congratulations to all of you."

Cassie glanced around, unsure of what to do now. She wasn't interested in talking to the press since they wanted to focus on her father instead of her. She spotted Beckett looking as shocked as she felt. She took a step toward the contractor and he flinched. She'd heard the vet had returned from Afghanistan with PTSD, but she hadn't seen evidence of it until now. He waved to her, so she approached him. "Congratulations, Beckett, on making the top five."

He stared at her for a moment and said, "Thanks. You, too."

"They paired you with Lauren Sterling, so you're in good hands."

He took a step away. "I guess." He glanced around at the group of people waiting to talk to them. "I gotta go." And he disappeared into the crowd.

The stage started to clear as Cassie turned to John. It probably wouldn't hurt to address one of the elephants in the room that stood between them. "What I said earlier about not wanting to work with you…"

He held up his hand. "I know you didn't mean it."

"But I did. Still do." She winced and tried to use better words. This wasn't the way to start a working relationship. "I hope that we can find a way to work with each other, because it's going to be a long, fruitless endeavor if we can't."

"I don't doubt that we can work together, Ms. Lowman. But I believe we both need to make a commitment to each other and this contest right now." He held out his hand. "I'm going to give my very best, and I hope you will, as well."

She shook his hand. "I never give anything less than all that I have."

With their hands clasped, she had the feeling that this was the beginning of something…different.

JOHN HELPED CASSIE off the platform, and the members of the press surrounded them, yelling questions and pushing in from all sides. When John had met Cassie earlier, he hadn't put her name together with the contractor who had been accused of embezzling from his own company though never proven. However, he couldn't hold her father's alleged crimes against her. If anything, it would bring more attention to them during the contest. Maybe they could come up with a strategy to use that to their advantage.

"Miss Lowman has no comment about her father at this time," John said into the microphone closest to him. "But we'd be happy to discuss making the top five teams tonight."

After a few moments of Cassie fielding inquiries about her experiences in rehabbing houses and him explaining his design credentials, the members of the press started to recede into the crowd. Clearly they weren't going to get the story they'd hoped for. Cassie turned to him. "Thank you for that. I still don't know what to say about my father."

He gave a shrug, as if it didn't matter. "This is about us, not him. And the sooner we established that with the press, the better."

But she still looked up at him as if he was a hero. Her two big friends approached them, and the slightly smaller one picked her up by the waist and swung her around. "I knew you could do this, kid."

She squealed and demanded that he put her down. Once on her feet, she waved her hand at them. "John, these are the Buttucci brothers Luigi and Mario. Better known as Biggie and Tiny. They are the best in the construction business I've ever known, and we're lucky that they're going to be working with us. They do everything: demolition, electrical, plumbing. But where they really shine is in painting. They don't need tape or edges. Steady hands, that's what they have."

John shook their hands in turn, wincing slightly at the pressure of each clasp. They seemed to be sending him a warning about not only themselves, but Cassie, too. He could see the protective stances they had with her, sandwiching her safely between them. He gave each of them a nod, hoping they could understand that he wanted only the best for their team. "It's great to meet you both."

They grunted, then looked back at Cassie. Tiny wiggled his eyebrows up and down. "Someone said you got the keys to the house. Wanna go see it now?"

It would be nice to get a sneak peek at the house that was going to consume all their attention for the next few months. John nodded. "I'm in."

They each drove their respective cars to the run-down neighborhood and parked on the curb under a tall oak tree that mirrored others that lined each side of the street. John stared up at the house, which seemed to have a small porch that listed to one side. Cassie took a few moments to change out of her heels and into work boots that she had apparently kept in her truck.

John was the first to walk up the cracked pathway to the small, rickety porch. He put a hand on a wrought iron column and winced as it shifted with very little pressure. He didn't need to have construction experience to realize what that probably meant. He turned to the trio behind him. "The porch's foundation is possibly an issue."

Cassie walked up the few steps and put the key in the lock, taking a deep breath before opening the door. She brought out her phone and turned on the flashlight feature. John mirrored her actions and shone his cell phone's light on the roof above the porch. Abandoned birds' nests, as well as cobwebs that spread their silky strands between joists, decorated the corners of the porch.

John hoped that the rest of the house would prove to be a diamond in the rough. They continued their tour. The carpet squished beneath their feet. Cassie bent down and touched the dampness. "Looks like we'll have plumbing issues, too. A burst pipe, maybe. Or looters stole the copper pipes." They walked into the kitchen. "And they stole the kitchen cabinets."

He stared at the exposed pipes and noted the sink was missing, too. What had he gotten himself into? He gave a shrug. "Well, on the bright side, that's less demolition we have to do."

"And the more we have to replace with an already limited budget." She brushed past him.

John stared out the window at the moonlit backyard full of weeds and overgrown grass. Another thing on their to-do list.

Cassie returned. "Four bedrooms that are in decent condition, but we're going to have to gut the bathroom." She crossed her arms and leaned against the wall. "I don't know what I expected, but it wasn't this."

"You're not giving up already, are you?"

She lifted her eyes to meet his, and her spine straightened. "Something you need to know about me. I don't ever give up. Got it?"

"Me, either."

At a loud noise from the living room, they rushed there to find Biggie standing knee-deep in a hole, having apparently crashed through the floor. John walked over and held out his hand to help him out.

Cassie squatted and peered at the floor, where a large gaping crater now yawned. "Definitely have to replace these floors."

John suddenly felt as if he was in way over his head.

CHAPTER TWO

THE OFFICES FOR the Belvedere Foundation were located in a skyscraper in downtown Detroit. Cassie had to pay ten dollars to park her truck in a multistory concrete lot. She hated to hand over the money but had given up trying to find a free, open spot on a side street.

She slammed the truck door shut, then looked down at her outfit. She didn't have to be as dressed up as she had the night before at the launch event, but she couldn't show up in her usual T-shirt and jeans, either. After consulting with her sister, she'd chosen a plain white cotton shirt and a pair of beige pants that her mother had probably stuffed in her closet at some point. It wasn't fancy, but she wanted to look as if she belonged.

Because despite everything that had

been printed about her in the morning paper, she deserved to be there. Didn't she?

Two security guards met her in the lobby of the glass-and-chrome skyscraper and directed her toward the Belvedere Foundation's boardroom, where the meeting was to be held. She felt tempted to pinch herself to make sure she wasn't dreaming all this. She'd really made it this far in the contest, and all that was left was to win the entire thing.

Opening the heavy door to the boardroom, she quickly scanned the crowd before she strode in with a confidence that she didn't quite feel. Better to fake it from the beginning. Some heads turned toward her, but then the people returned to their conversations. Ignoring the dismissal, she tried to focus on the advice Andie had given her over the phone that morning. "You earned your place, Cass. Don't let them take it from you. Instead, you show them what we Lowmans are made of. Grit and determination."

"Grit and determination," Cassie mumbled under her breath as she squared her shoulders and headed for a long, narrow table to the side, set with a continental breakfast. She loaded her plate with fresh fruit and a cinnamon roll rivaling the size of her head, before she moved down the table to the large carafes that held coffee and hot water for tea. She poured a mug and held it up to her face, inhaling the heady scent of coffee beans. Ah, ambrosia for her soul.

"Hey, partner."

John was pouring his own cup of coffee. "Good morning to you. How did you sleep?"

He gave her a wry grin and shrugged. "I couldn't sleep. I had so many ideas bubbling in my brain that I stayed up late drawing different sketches of the house."

"Sketches are good."

He took a long sip of coffee, then sighed. "We're going to need a coffee maker at the house since I subsist on caffeine and pizza. And that's on a good day."

She laughed and nodded. "Me, too." She had an old percolator that she was in the habit of hauling to each work site because she couldn't get through her day without regular infusions of caffeine.

"Well, we have one thing in common at least." He glanced at the others in the room. "Is it just me or do you feel like we're the underdogs in this contest? That the contestants have dismissed us already as competitors?"

It was what had kept her up the night before, tossing and turning as she mulled over her doubts. True, she had made it this far, but now what? She felt as if she and John had lost already before the contest had even started. "You're not imagining that. I feel it, too."

She noticed his brown eyes held a golden gleam in them. "We could use that to our advantage, you know. Let them underestimate us. And in the meantime, we'll swoop in and take the top prize."

She wished she had such confidence. "Do you really think we could win?"

Before he could answer, Christopher Belvedere swept through the door, flanked by a pair of assistants presumably, and called for everyone's attention. The rest of the contestants took seats around the main table that dominated the room. John found them two available seats and used his free hand to pull her chair out for her before sitting down himself. Mr. Belvedere stood at a lectern at one end of the table. "Good morning, ladies and gentlemen. If we could all listen up, we can begin this first meeting." He nodded at his assistants. "We're passing around information sheets with the rules and regulations for the contest. Much of this is a repeat of what we discussed during your interviews, but I'd like to go over each item and address any questions."

A thick sheaf of papers was dropped down on the table, next to Cassie's plate. She skimmed the first page as she bit into a fresh strawberry. Most of the text was standard rules and regulations for renovating a house. Permits would be pulled, inspections made regularly. She didn't have a chance to read it all before Mr. Belvedere started talking.

"First, let me congratulate you all on being chosen. You are all part of an elite group of builders and designers, the cream of the crop in Detroit."

The affirmation made Cassie's heart want to sing out. See that? She was special.

"Second, since this is the premier contest there may be unexpected challenges for you and us as we navigate these un-chartered waters. The mayor has assured us that he will assist us in the necessary bu-reaucracy of the city's agencies. That being said, I am also here to help you in getting permits arranged, inspections cleared, and so on. Do not hesitate to reach out to me or my office."

Seated across the table from Cassie, Beckett raised his hand. "I have a question about the security of these houses. Is there anything in place to protect our work?"

Mr. Belvedere cleared his throat and spoke again. "All of you were chosen not only for your talent and skills but also for your integrity. We have confidence that no one will be stealing ideas or anything else."

Several people turned to look at Cassie, and she bristled under the attention. She wasn't here to take something that didn't belong to her, but to prove that she had what it took to keep her father's business going until he returned and was exoner-ated. She shook her head and muttered, "Why do I feel like there's a target on my back?"

John inclined his head toward hers and whispered, "Like I said, we should use that to our advantage."

The meeting continued as they reviewed the packet of information, including a list of vendors who were helping to sponsor the contest and would provide deep discounts. She perused the names and gave a nod. She knew many of them from previous jobs, so she could vouch for the quality of their materials.

The doors to the boardroom opened, and several assistants walked in with large cardboard boxes. Mr. Belvedere smirked. "And here is our first challenge in the contest. As you know, homes are getting smarter as more technology is used to enhance the lives of those who live there. We want these homes to use cutting-edge digital devices to make them safer as well as more practical. In each box, you will find a suite of technology to be incorporated into your projects. Home connectivity and security systems that will bring these residences into the twenty-first century. This is a step up from current systems sold, the next generation of symbiotic connectivity. With this technology, the families that move into your homes will be able to make their lives easier with a simple spoken command."

A box was placed in front of Cassie and John. She rose to her feet and opened the lid, groaning at the sight of a bunch of computerized circuitry. She'd never been good at this part of the job. Give her a piece of pipe to replace or a socket to install, any day. But electronics and cable? She shuddered at the thought.

John stood next to her and perused the items in the box, as well, and shrugged. "I installed my own home sound system, so maybe I can help the experts. Won't we have to plan where we want the walls before the cables can be placed correctly?"

"Yes. And, how will all this fit in with your ideas?"

He stared at her, and she swallowed her irritation. His eyes didn't waver or show any doubt as he answered, "We'll make it work."

She nodded and sat back down.

Mr. Belvedere tapped a pen on the lectern. "We'll have more challenges as we go along, and I look forward to seeing how you incorporate them into your designs. In the near future, you will also be assigned a family who will be gifted the home at the end of the contest, so keep that in mind as you design."

He wished them good luck, reminded them of the three-month deadline and left the room.

John packed everything back into the box and placed the lid on top. He checked his watch before his gaze landed on her. "Do you have plans now? I thought we should go over some of the sketches and get a jump on where to start."

"I'm all yours." She frowned at how that sounded. "I mean, I'm free. Do you want to go to the house to do that? We need to start determining what stays and what goes before demolition tomorrow."

He finished his coffee, then placed the empty cup on the table. "No, I want to get some real food. Do you know Lolly's on Grand Boulevard? We could meet there and have lunch."

"Great," she replied, following him as he carried the tech box out of the building.

JOHN HELD THE door to the diner open for Cassie, and they took a booth near the back. He waved to a waitress, who brought over a full carafe of coffee and placed it on a ceramic stone in the center of the table. "Ah, Marie, you know me so well. Leave your no-good husband and marry me instead."

She laughed as she poured the first mug and handed it to him. "You couldn't afford me."

He took a quick sip of the black brew. "You spoil me, so I'd have to find a way to treat you well. Even if it meant robbing a bank."

She hit him on the shoulder with a plastic menu before placing it in front of him. He chuckled as Marie handed a menu to Cassie, who was staring at him, eyebrows raised. "I take it they know you here."

"I'm a bachelor who lives around the corner and eats most of my meals at Lolly's." Relaxed, he put his arms across the back of the booth. "I couldn't ask for a better kitchen."

Cassie shook her head and opened the menu.

Once they ordered, John took his time

stirring cream into his coffee, focusing on each turn of the spoon. The clink it made as it hit the side of the mug. The milk-scented steam rising. The dark brown swirling into an ecru. It was almost like a ritual before he brought the cup to his lips and sipped from it. He sighed in appreciation.

"You weren't kidding when you said you like coffee."

"Nope." He took another sip and closed his eyes. "And I'll need lots of it to do my best work."

Cassie laid her hands on the table. "Before we get into the nuts and bolts of what we're about to do, I have a question for you. Why did you enter the contest?"

"I needed a new challenge and a new career. This contest seemed to provide both." He eyed her over the coffee mug. "What about you? Why did you enter the contest?"

"When we win, I'm going to use the money and the publicity to bring back Lowman Construction to what it once was."

John gave a whistle. "When we win, huh? I like the sound of that. Which reminds me..." He brought out his sketchbook, flipped through a few pages and laid it open on the table. "This is a rough idea of the current floor plan. It will help me to stay focused on the space available." He pointed to a page and slid the book closer to Cassie. "This is what I'm thinking for the kitchen."

Cassie looked up from the book. "The kitchen? The living room's not the priority?"

"Kitchens are where everyone spends most of their time, right?"

He turned to another page. "Without cabinets and a sink already in place, we can design the kitchen however we wish, from top to bottom. I saw this farmhouse sink at a salvage yard that would be perfect, and I thought that—"

She held up a hand. "Who said anything about a salvage yard?"

"Me. Just now."

"I'm not putting junk in our house."

"I didn't say anything about junk." He pointed to the sketch of the sink he'd drawn from memory. "This is a good-quality piece that just needs a good home. And it'll cost a lot less than any we'd find at those pricey vendors on the list."

"I'm not putting anything used in our house. We need new, quality materials that will put us over the top. Don't you want to win?"

"Let's face it. I didn't enter the contest to lose, and neither did you. " He glanced up as Marie placed their meals in front of them and he thanked her. "Cassie, I think that this could give us an edge over our competitors. Repurposing what we can and finding salvaged pieces where we can't. Everyone else can be slightly different versions of each other, but we'll be unique."

Cassie shook her head. "No, we'll look as if we bought our supplies at a garage sale. My dad would never have done that."

"Do you always do what your dad would have wanted? You can't honestly be that naive." He grabbed up his soupspoon, but then paused. "Haven't you done any research? Salvaging is a big trend, and it's one I want to incorporate into my ideas."

"Don't forget that they may be your ideas, but it's our house. I have a say in this, too." She picked at her sandwich. "I've never worked with salvaged materials," she mumbled.

"Is that why you're afraid to try them?"

She raised her head to glare at him. "I'm not afraid."

She might have said the words, but the quaver in her voice told him that she probably wrestled with the same fears that had kept him up the night before. "Aren't you? You have a lot riding on this contest."

"As do you."

He nodded and leaned forward. "Exactly. This is why I want to step out of the cookie-cutter mold everyone else will use and do something different."

She plucked a piece of bacon from the BLT and stuffed it in her mouth. He could almost see the gears in her brain working as she chewed. Finally she swallowed and turned to another page of his sketchbook. "I'm willing to consider it. Now what's this?"

He ran a finger along the edge of the picture. He'd thought of this when he remembered his grandmother's house and drawing pictures at the kitchen table when he was about six years old. "That's the window in the breakfast nook. I'd like to turn it into a window seat, which will save space and provide storage beneath it."

"Now, that I like."

They flipped through more sketches, and she commented on several. Reaching the last of them, she gave a nod. "You do have some good ideas."

"But you're not sold on them yet."

"No." She fidgeted with her napkin. "John, this contest means I can turn my father's company into my own. We need to be number one. Second place still makes us losers."

He reached over and put his hand on top of hers, stilling it for a moment. "This is my second chance at finding my life's work. It used to be cars, but getting laid off made me realize that I was ready for a change. Something that will bring back that love of design. I want this as much as you do."

She removed her hand from his. "I understand. More than you know."

AFTER LUNCH, BACK at the house, Cassie stared up at the next three months of her life, dilapidated as it was. In the light of day, the home looked worse than she had remembered it. Could she and John and the Buttuccis do as the Belvedere Foundation wanted and find the jewel underneath the rubble?

John walked up behind her. "I don't remember it looking so abandoned and sad last night."

"Dusk can hide a lot of flaws." She held up the key to the front door. "Let's take our time and do another walk-through."

"Let me grab my sketchbook." He left her and retrieved it from the front seat of his car along with a tin that held his charcoal pencils. "I want to do a quick sketch of the exterior before we go in."

She pointed at the blank page and then at him. "You draw. I'm going in."

But he was already absorbed in getting the lines of the house drawn on paper. She noticed the weeds growing from between the cement slabs. How much of their budget could they allocate to landscaping? Much of the neglect only needed some muscle to fix, which wouldn't cost anything but several hours. She put a hand on the overgrown browning shrubs that flanked the front porch. Some pruning might bring them back to life.

She glanced behind her. John was frowning as he continued to sketch. Was he seeing the same neglect that she saw? Or did his artistic eye see possibilities that she couldn't get to yet? Shaking off the thoughts, she unlocked the front door and stepped inside.

The hole where Biggie had fallen through the floor to the ground gaped at her as if it, too, was surprised to find itself there. She knelt and stared down at the crawl space revealed below. If the house had sat on a basement, he would have fallen through the rotting floor at least ten feet instead of only the few that he had. The damp wood along the jagged edges seemed to indicate it was more a cause of rotting wood rather than the foundation. Thankfully, it might mean the problem was limited to the living room and did not pervade the entire house.

The front door swung open and John breezed in with his sketchbook. He groaned at the hole. "I'd almost forgotten about that."

Cassie put her hands on her knees and pushed herself to a standing position. "I wish I had. We'll have to walk carefully in this room until we know for sure how much of the floorboards have rotted. I don't know if it's extended to the bedrooms or not."

He nodded and took careful steps toward the hall that led to the bedrooms and bathroom. "The layout looks smaller than I remember."

"It was probably made in the years immediately after World War II, when houses were built quickly and with only the basic needs in mind. My guess is that we have about fifteen hundred square feet. Eighteen hundred, if we're lucky." She knelt and touched the green shag carpet in the hallway. "It's not damp here, so we might be okay with the floors through the rest of the house."

John drew more lines and curves on the page before moving into one of the bedrooms. "I wonder if we could get a hold of the original blueprints for this place."

"Maybe." She opened the folding closet door. "We could probably check the attic." She pointed to a covered access point. "I can grab my ladder from the truck if we want to go up now."

"With all the spiders and creepy crawlies, not to mention dust and cobwebs?" He shuddered and gave a grimace. "I'll wait until we're dressed more appropriately."

"Chicken."

He waggled his eyebrows and walked across the hall to the bathroom, which sported avocado green and harvest gold tiles. Based on the colors, style and condition, she figured it had been renovated in the 1970s. John frowned. "You don't see a green toilet very often."

"Don't forget the matching avocado bathtub." She put a hand on the shower rod and gave it a tug. It didn't budge, and she figured that meant the tiles and fixtures would be harder to remove. "We'll need to replace all of this. I'm thinking a fiberglass shower enclosure and bathtub. Maybe a low-flush toilet. Pedestal sink."

"Maybe."

She raised her eyebrows at this. "You want to keep green and gold?"

He shuddered much as he had at the mention of spiders. "I like the green. Maybe combine it with a color like ecru to make it more earthy. More Zen. And a pedestal sink won't give much storage in an already cramped space."

"Yes, but it will open up the look of the room more than a cabinet with a sink would."

"Maybe."

She put her hands on her hips and stared at him. "Do you plan on disagreeing with everything I say?"

"I'm leaving us open to options right now."

"Mmm-hmm."

Back in the kitchen, they peered at the walls. She said, "The age of the house could be to our advantage because the structure was built to last. If we gut it to the studs, we can open things up and make it look bigger."

"What about removing the wall between here and the living room? So that it's more like one large room rather than two? Maybe like this." He sketched a quick floor plan to demonstrate what he meant.

Cassie put her hand on the doorjamb and looked up at the ceiling. "That could be a load-bearing wall, so we'll have to take that into consideration. But I can see what you mean. I like it."

He grinned and walked toward the kitchen window, tucking the sketchpad under his arm. "So when do we start?"

"We'll start demolition tomorrow, especially on the bathroom. Tear up the floor in the living room. Take the walls down to the studs to see what we're working with underneath. And then what comes after that depends on you and your designs."

The cell phone in her front pants pocket started to vibrate. She pulled it out and stared at the number on the display. It wasn't one that she recognized. Tempted to let the call go to voice mail, she changed her mind suddenly and swiped to the right to answer it. "Lowman Construction."

"Cass."

Her father.

She held her breath, not knowing what to say. She hadn't heard from him in almost a year, since the day before he disappeared. They'd been working on a job site, and he'd said good-night to her as she always did while she stayed behind to secure it before going home herself. There'd been no indication he was about to flee. No hint that he was even under investigation. She noticed John, so she stepped into the living room for privacy.

"Cass, you don't really think a contest is going to help, do you? I wouldn't have done it."

"You didn't give me much of a choice. It will help me get the company back." She blinked quickly to keep the tears from falling. "Daddy, where are you?"

Silence. She held the phone away from her to see that he'd already hung up. She checked her call history and pressed her finger to the last number received. But it only rang until she gave up.

CHAPTER THREE

CASSIE NOTED THE time on her truck's dashboard and swallowed a curse. She'd promised her mother she'd be on time for dinner for once, but she was late by ten minutes already. She could blame the traffic for the delay, but the new house had eaten up her day.

After the phone call from her father, she'd allowed herself only five minutes to ruminate before switching her attention back to the project. If John noticed she was distracted even for a short while, he refrained from mentioning it.

She pulled into her mother's driveway and stopped behind her sister's sleek sports car. A quick glance in the rearview mirror revealed that her hair looked as if she'd brushed it that morning and had done nothing to it since then. It was her usual MO. She wasn't one to waste minutes on her appearance beyond what was necessary. She took in her white shirt and frowned at the smear of something that she had brushed against while she and John discussed plans for their house.

Their house. It almost sounded as if they were a couple. Not that she'd mind if those golden brown eyes of his turned in her direction with something akin to admiration. Or that generous mouth of his did something besides make impossible suggestions or logically reject her ideas.

The front door opened, and her mother stood in the doorway peering at her. Best get inside and take her lumps. She got out of the truck, walked up to her mother and gave her a quick kiss on her cheek. "Sorry I'm late."

"Your sister arrived ten minutes early."

Of course, she had. Andie was never late for anything. "I was at the house with my partner, John."

Her sister gave her a swift hug. "I saw his picture next to yours in the paper. Quite a dish. Think you'll introduce me?"

Cassie gave her sister a once-over. Andie wore a cream lace top over moss green linen pants that refused to wrinkle. Her long dark hair was swept up in a ponytail with not a strand out of place. How did she make gorgeous look so easy? If John saw her, Cassie would never get a chance.

Not that she was looking for one. They had to work together. Anything else would just complicate matters.

She shrugged. "I'm sure you'll meet eventually. You could drop by the house once we begin the demo."

Andie wrinkled her nose. "And get sawdust all over my clothes?" She shuddered, then laughed. "But for a good-looking man, I might take that risk."

Right. Her sister couldn't get dirty, which is why she'd been the receptionist at her father's office instead of being on-site. Cassie sniffed the air and grinned. "You made shepherd's pie?" It was her favorite as well as her father's.

"It's been awhile since we've had it," her mother said.

Since her father had disappeared last summer. Had her mom received a call from him, too?

Her mother led them into the dining

room, which was already set with china and crystal. Her mother believed that every day was a cause to celebrate, so they used the good stuff on a regular basis. She motioned for her and Andie to take their usual places on either side of the table, seating herself at the end. Conversation waited while they filled their plates with the casserole, salad and rolls.

It seemed like lunch with John had been a decade ago rather than six hours. She couldn't seem to get the food in fast enough, and she stopped momentarily to see her mother watching her with a wrinkle in her brow. Cassie put her fork down. "Sorry. I guess I was hungry."

Her mother sighed and took a sip of wine from her glass. "I saw the write-up for the contest in the paper this morning."

The hidden message being Cassie hadn't called her with the news first. "I didn't get home until late, then I had an early meeting at the Belvedere Foundation this morning."

"So what's the house like?" Andie asked as she buttered her roll.

How to describe the disaster? "Old and out-of-date. Run down from neglect and abandonment. But there's potential there. I think we could really make something of this place."

"You sound like your father when he started a job."

Cassie glanced at her mother. "That's good, right?"

Her mother made a face as if to dismiss the words. A look of pain entered her mother's features before she took another sip of wine. If Cassie missed her father, how much more had her mother missed him? She never talked about it, but it had to have taken a toll. Especially while being under the scrutiny of the police. None of them had any answers at the time of his disappearance, much less after almost a year.

Cassie looked down at her plate, wondering if she should bring up her father's call. It had been short, almost nothing. Less than sixty seconds. But it had stirred something in her. Something she needed to say aloud to her family, if no one else. She took a deep breath and turned to her mother. "He called me."

Andie gasped and put a hand to her

mouth while her mother set her wine glass on the table and leaned forward. "When?"

"This afternoon." Cassie pulled the cell phone from her pants pocket and put it on the table. "He criticized me for entering the contest. That was it, then he was gone."

Her mother's jaw clenched and unclenched. "You need to tell the police."

"I know, but—"

Her mother's expression was one of total fury. "Cassandra Jane, you need to tell them. We can't keep something like this from them."

"There's not much to tell, Mom. I tried calling the number back, but it keeps ringing." She unlocked the phone and showed the call history. Seven times she'd called. And seven times he hadn't answered.

Her mother rose to her feet and left the dining room. Andromeda took the phone from Cassie. She ran her finger over the display, pressed the number and placed the phone to her ear.

Cassie reached out for the cell, but her sister held it away from her. "I told you, he didn't answer any of my calls."

After a moment, Andie nodded and

handed her the phone. "He knew about the contest. That must mean he's in the area still."

"Or he's keeping track of us online. It's not like you have to be in Detroit to know what's going on."

"He's watching over you at least. He's never called me."

The bitterness in her sister's words mirrored the sour look on her face. She placed her napkin beside her plate, then left.

Cassie glanced around the empty room. Despite the beautiful place settings and the delicious food, ugliness had found its way to mar the family dinner. She soon found her mother and sister in the backyard, her sister leaning against the deck railing while her mother walked along the perimeter of the yard pulling at weeds. Andie put a hand on Cassie's arm when she started down the steps to join her mother. "Let her grieve."

"He's not dead."

"He's not coming back, so he might as well be."

Cassie shook off her sister's hand and met her mother by the lilac bush that had been planted there when she was born.

She'd always thought of it as hers because of that. Now she snapped off a fragrant bloom and held it out to her mother. "I'm sorry."

Closing her eyes, her mother held up the flower to her nose and took a deep breath. She reached out and patted Cassie's shoulder. "It's your father's fault, not yours. He's the one who got into this mess."

"I'll contact the detective to let him know Daddy called me."

"It's the right thing to do, Cassandra." She looked up at the house. "The lawyer thinks we may have to sell the place to pay back the missing money that your father took."

Andie joined them. "We didn't take the money, so why should we pay it back?"

Cassie knew that even if they got top dollar, the sale of the house wouldn't be enough to pay back everyone in full. More than half a million dollars was missing from the company's accounts. "When were you going to tell us this?"

Their mother shook her head. "When I knew something more definite. Why get you upset over something that might not happen? I've been thinking about calling a Realtor to put it on the market."

"If you do sell the house, where will you go?" Cassie asked.

Andie glanced at her, but Cassie shook her head. "My house is still under construction."

"It's been that way since you bought it two years ago. When are you planning on finishing it?" her sister scolded.

As soon as she had more money. She'd started renovating it right after she'd moved in, but the funds had dried up after the first year. Now she fixed things as time and money allowed. It was livable for her, but her mother had higher standards. Like a kitchen that had walls besides studs. "Mother could stay with you at your apartment."

"On the pull-out sofa? I don't think so."

"Girls, I appreciate the offers but I'll figure something out myself." She put a hand on first Andromeda's cheek, then Cassandra's. "We'll get through this like we have everything else."

In Cassie's mind, they'd gotten through it by not talking about it. At all. One day, her father had been there. The next, he hadn't been, along with the half a million according to the detective assigned to the case. She had been questioned since she was directly involved with the construction business, but it became clear she had no idea where her father was or what he had done. She didn't believe he could do the things they blamed him for. Her father was no thief, but she didn't have an explanation for the missing money. His disappearance only added weight to their accusations.

Cassie slapped at a mosquito that nibbled on her wrist. "We still don't know for sure that it was Daddy who took the money."

Andie gave her a scowl and turned back to the house. Cassie knew that her sister never doubted that their father was guilty of everything that the detectives had accused him of. But she had her reservations. Daddy wouldn't steal from his own company, much less the clients who were the lifeblood of their business. He wouldn't do that to her. She'd hoped to keep the business running after he retired in the next ten years or so. Yet, there were times she wondered if he could have done it. If he had.

Her mother looked even sadder than before as she put a hand on Cassie's shoulder. "Cassandra…" She blinked and then gave a quick shake of her head. "Let's go finish dinner. We'll talk about this later."

Cassie watched her retreat. She doubted they would talk. Though part of her needed to get these fears and doubts off her chest. To share what had kept her awake at night.

But she was a Lowman. And her family didn't speak about unpleasant topics if they could be avoided.

Cassie slapped at another mosquito and joined her family inside the dining room, where they resumed eating. She took her seat and placed the napkin back on her lap, picked up her fork and dragged it through the mashed potato crust of the shepherd's pie. She was no longer hungry.

BEFORE HEADING TO the house for the first day of demolition, John picked up coffees for the team. Not sure how they liked to drink it, he asked for packets of cream and sugar on the side. Because of his stop, he was the last to arrive. Cassie's truck had the tailgate down. He picked up the cardboard carrier, carefully removed himself from the car and approached the house. One of the Buttucci brothers walked out of the open doorway and grunted a welcome. John held up the carrier. "I brought liquid motivation"

Biggie took one cup with a murmur of thanks and continued his journey to the truck to grab a sledgehammer. John followed him inside and grimaced at the hole in the floor that seemed to gape even wider. "Good morning," he called down the hallway, where he could hear voices drifting out of the bathroom.

Cassie appeared and held up her hand in greeting. "John, I wasn't expecting you this early."

A horse of a dog galloped into the living room from the kitchen and stood between him and Cassie. John took a step back. Cassie put a hand in the dog's blond fur. "This is Evie. She's a Belgian Bouvier de Flandres, so she thinks she's my protector."

"You bring your dog to the work site?"

"She's well trained, and I'll keep her in the backyard." Cassie shrugged. "She wouldn't have it any other way. Besides,

I work long hours on a job and it's nice to have someone who thinks she's tougher than she is to keep me safe. Do you have a problem with that?" She looked him over and he wondered if he'd worn something wrong. "Why are you here for the demolition? Shouldn't you be home drawing up sketches or something?"

"You don't think I can help you tear out tile and rotten wood planks?" He held out a cup of coffee to her. "I can do this." Biggie hefted the sledgehammer over his shoulder. John gave a nod. "I'm part of this team, and I'd appreciate it if you would include me."

"Suit yourself." She took the cup and held it up in salute. "Thanks. I brought my coffee maker but forgot the beans. I'll pick some up during our lunch break."

Tiny joined them. "George is renovating the house across the street and said the dumpsters are being delivered later this morning. We'll have to remove the debris and put it in the front yard for now."

"Actually, I have an idea about that. I'd like to use some of the broken tiles in a mosaic." John quickly tore a piece off a paper bag that held supplies. He removed the pencil from the back pocket of his jeans and drew an outline of a star divided into smaller squares and triangles. "I was thinking we could reuse the tile to create something to hang on the wall or maybe a patio table for the backyard."

"In avocado and gold?" Cassie shook her head. "I don't know about that. Not exactly a winning color combination."

She had a point. "Are there any rules that say we can't use what other teams are throwing out? I might be able to get more tiles in other colors that way."

Tiny looked skeptically at his brother. "We're decorating with trash now?" he asked.

"We're salvaging what we can. The Belvedere Foundation said we had hidden gems here in this neighborhood. Why not carry out that theme in the decor too?" John knew he had a great idea, but the other three didn't look convinced. "What would it hurt to let me try this?"

Cassie glared at him. "We're limited on time as it is."

"I'll work on it during my free time." Granted, he had the same twenty-four hours in a day that everyone else was allotted, but he'd find time to work on something that had meaning to him.

He could practically see the gears turning in Cassie's brain before she gave a short nod. "Do what you want. But if it doesn't work out, it doesn't stay in the design."

"Agreed."

Biggie seemed to have a gleam in his eye as he took the sledgehammer and headed down the hallway to the bathroom. In a few seconds, a loud crash followed by the tinkle of broken tiles hitting the floor filled the quiet. Cassie smiled and rubbed her hands together. "Here's to the start of a beautiful home."

John looked around. "What would you have me do?"

"Find a pair of gloves and start placing the broken tiles and plaster in one of the empty bins I brought. When it's full, place the bin outside." She slipped a pair of goggles over her eyes and put on her own pair of gloves. "Tiny and I are tearing up carpet."

He found an empty bin in the kitchen along with other supplies, including an extra pair of work gloves. He'd have to go and get some of his own soon if he wanted to continue this new career. Putting them on, he skirted around Cassie, who was pulling up the soggy shag carpet in the living room. She moaned as she saw the ruined wood floor underneath. "There's nothing to save here."

Tiny agreed. "Maybe it'll be okay in the bedrooms."

"If we're lucky."

John met Biggie in the bathroom. The big man gave a grunt and smashed the sledgehammer between the bathtub and toilet. John scooped up debris and put it in the bin and smiled to himself when Biggie hefted the sledgehammer over his shoulder and brought it down with force against the wall.

"You like that, don't you?"

Biggie nodded and continued to smash tile. John filled one bin, took it outside and exchanged it for another empty one. As he walked back through the house, he watched Tiny roll the last of the carpet into one long, wet roll and throw it over his shoulder. Cassie yanked a bandanna from her back pocket and wiped her forehead before tying it around her hair. "I'll have to bring fans tomorrow to keep us cool while we're working if this heat continues."

"It should. It's the end of May."

"You never know. It's also Michigan, so we could get a cold front at any moment." She stared at John, her head cocked to one side. "You might not want to wear your best pair of jeans for this job. Especially during demo."

John looked down at his pants. "This isn't my best pair."

"I'm just saying you're not going to want to wear nice clothes when we're at these beginning stages. If ever." She pulled at the edge of her tank top. "I can't tell you how many times I've had to replace these because of paint splatter or because of rips and tears."

"I get it, Cassie."

She watched him for a moment and then nodded. "I know."

But her expression at what he wore made him think she did believe him to be slightly clueless. He swallowed a rebuke and returned to the bathroom, where Biggie sat on the edge of the tub, wiping his forehead with a rag. John bent and started putting more debris into the bin. Biggie stood and put a hand on John's shoulder, making him look up. "She's only looking out for you, you know?"

Surprised the big man could be soft-spoken, John nodded and returned to his job.

THE DUMPSTER ARRIVED and was positioned between their house and the one next door, which was assigned to Butler Construction. Cassie wheeled the first bin of debris to dump into the huge receptacle and almost stumbled over Nick, one of her competitors. He tossed an armful of rotten wood panels into the dumpster, then watched her empty the bin from her side.

"Congratulations on being one of the finalists," he offered.

"You, too. But then I figured you were a shoo-in."

He grinned. "Well, I don't mean to toot my own horn, but my brothers and I also landed a huge contract for a subdivision."

The crown jewel for a contractor. A subdivision meant years of steady work and income. Her father hadn't had a contract like that for a while. "That's great, Nick. Will your brothers be able to do it on their own with you here?"

"They'll keep me in the loop until the contest is over." He looked behind her toward her house. "Is yours as big of a nightmare as ours?"

She didn't want to give too much of their situation away to a fellow competitor. Better to keep certain things to herself for now. "I've seen worse, but we'll be fine. My designer has a lot of big ideas."

"The car guy? No offense, Cass, but what does he know about designing a home?"

Hearing him voice her own doubts about John raised her hackles. "Knows a lot more than Tiffany, whose idea of high concept is open space filled with tchotchkes and knickknacks."

Nick bristled at the insult to his partner's design ideas and left. Okay, so maybe she shouldn't have antagonized the first contractor to have been nice to her. But then, he'd tried to make her doubt John's abilities, and for better or worse they were a team. She turned to find John holding a rolled-up piece of carpet on his shoulder. She wondered how much of the conversation he'd heard.

He threw the carpet into the dumpster. "You shouldn't be fraternizing with the enemy. He's trying to get under your skin and undermine your confidence…"

"I know he is."

"…and to make me look like the reason you'll lose."

The truth was, some of John's ideas had already made her wonder if she'd been paired with the wrong person. She needed to win this contest, and that meant having a designer who would knock the socks off the judges. She wasn't yet convinced that John was that person. She pointed at him. "You better not let me down."

"Back at you." He turned on his heel but paused, then continued down the sidewalk past other homes in the neighborhood.

Where was he going? They had work to do, and he was choosing to go on a stroll? Now? She shook her head and pushed the bin back to the house. Tiny sat on an upside-down garbage can, chugging a bottle of water. He finished and gestured behind her. "Where's John?"

"Went for a walk."

Tiny gave her a look. "What did you say to him?"

She held out her hands at her sides. "How do you know it's what I said?"

"Because if he said something goofy to you, you'd be the one walking around the neighborhood to calm your temper."

"I told him not to let me down."

Tiny removed his ball cap and scratched at his balding head. "Isn't it kind of early to start doubting his abilities?"

She knew he was right, but she wasn't ready to concede just yet. "I haven't seen much of his abilities beyond pencil sketches and ideas to use trash to make wall hangings."

"And you wonder why he walked off?"

She sighed and leaned on the doorframe to the kitchen. "I need this win. We all do if we want to keep Daddy's company going."

"It'll take more than winning a contest for that to happen, sweetie, and you know it."

Tiny didn't understand. No one seemed

to. Winning meant she could prove to everyone that she was just as good a builder as her father. And maybe prove it to herself. If she won, that would mean restarting Lowman Construction under her management. She could be what she'd always wanted—her own boss. Was it too much to ask for?

JOHN GOT TO the end of the street before it ended at the large avenue, crossed and started his trek back. What had he been thinking? Was this contest really the answer to his worries? He'd been lost and floundering, unsure of what to do next. The announcement by the Belvedere Foundation seemed to be the solution he'd been waiting for. What if it hadn't been? What if he had put all his hopes in something that would lead to nothing? If they won, his designs would be seen across the country. With that kind of exposure and his half of the quarter of a million dollars, he could start his own business. They'd be his own deadlines rather than having to answer to a supervisor who left things to the last minute and expected him to accomplish the impossible.

He passed several more homes and slowed his pace. These ones sat closer to the main road and seemed older and more unique than the cookie-cutter-style homes at the other end that they were renovating. His fingers itched, and he wished that he'd brought his sketchpad. That and water, since the day was so warm. He stopped to wipe his forehead, then peered up at the scorching sun.

"You look like you could use a drink of water, young man."

John shielded his eyes to see where the voice had come from. An older woman, fanning herself, was sitting on a wooden glider on a covered porch. He walked up the short path to her house. "Yes, ma'am. It's a hot one today."

She pointed at the porch steps. "You stay there. I'll be right back."

He put a foot on the first step and waited. The woman returned with a glass of water that had about a dozen cubes of ice floating in it.

"Thank you, ma'am." He took a long

drink, then placed the cool glass against his sweaty forehead. "That hits the spot."

She gave a wave of her hand. "Call me Loretta."

"And I'm John."

She motioned to a wicker chair that sported a crocheted pillow on the seat. "You might as well sit while you finish your drink."

He sat down, took another long pull of the cold water and let out a sigh. "Thank you for this. I should have brought water on my walk."

"Where you walking to?"

He shrugged. "Nowhere. I needed to clear my head before I said some things better left unsaid."

She winked. "Problem with a woman?"

"Not in the way you're thinking." He looked up at the ceiling of the porch, where someone had painted a rainbow. "Who's the artist?"

"My granddaughter thought it needed some sprucing up. And I'm getting too old to be climbing on ladders to paint a porch that is exposed to the elements."

"She's got talent."

The woman smiled. "You one of those contest people?"

"Yes. I'm a designer."

"When they announced the contest, there were folks around here who worried about what that meant for our little neighborhood. They like the quiet and what's familiar. Me? I miss the young families that brought the noise only children could bring." She leaned forward on the glider. "Do you think they'll sell those houses to families?"

"I believe they are being given to deserving families. They haven't shared many details on that so far."

She nodded again and looked out at the houses that lined the street. "When things got bad, people losing their jobs and their homes, half the neighborhood disappeared." She put a hand to her lips, shaking her head. "There's only a bunch of us left now."

"How long have you lived here?"

"Since my Walter came home from Vietnam and asked me to marry him. This was his mama's house." She set the glider to rocking. "Almost fifty good years we've had here. My daughter keeps talking about selling up and moving us to one of those assisted living places. I don't want to give up my home. It don't matter how convenient it is for her to have us there. It's not convenient for me."

"Do you know when the house was built?"

"Walter's granddad built it from a kit he bought from Sears. Can you believe that?" She laughed and shook her head.

John had figured it might have been a Craftsman home and longed to see what it looked like inside. But his mom had taught him manners, so he didn't invite himself in. Instead, he finished his water and held out the empty glass to Loretta. "Thank you for the drink. I need to get back to work."

"Which house is yours?"

"Number 2905."

She grinned. "The Czarnecks used to live there. I remember their green and yellow bathroom." She made a face. "There's no accounting for some people's tastes." She stood as he did so. "On your next break, stop back here. I might have some pictures of the neighborhood from the old days."

"I'd appreciate that, Miss Loretta."

She walked him to the edge of the porch. "Are all the people in this contest as polite as you?"

"I'm one of a kind."

"That you are, John. A pleasure to meet you."

"Likewise."

He stepped off the porch and waved once he reached the sidewalk. When he returned to the house, he located Cassie sitting on the floor, her legs dangling in the hole. She looked up at him as he entered. "You're back." He nodded and looked around for the brothers. "They left to pick up lunch for us."

He gestured to the hole. "You thinking of keeping it there?"

She smiled and shook her head. "Nope. Just thinking."

He took a seat next to her and dangled his legs close to hers. "I want to win this contest, but that means working together, not arguing. That applies to both of us."

"I really need this, John."

Her eyes were dewy with moisture. The vulnerability he saw made him want to put his arms around her, to whisper into her hair that everything would be okay. Instead, he sat quietly next to her and let her think.

Finally, she gave a deep sigh. "We should get moving. Sitting here and hoping for things to be different isn't going to win this contest."

When she started to stand, John tugged on her hand. "Cassie, for better or worse we're a team, and we need to start acting like one. You need my input for the construction just as I need yours for the design. We have to do this together. I need to know I can rely on you. And let me reassure you that you can depend on me."

She stared at their joined hands. "The only one I've ever depended on was my dad. And you know how that turned out. Trust has to be earned."

She took a step back and started to walk into the kitchen but turned back. "I want to trust you, John. I'm just scared to."

He stood and winced at the tearing sound. He reached behind and felt where his jeans had ripped thanks to the jagged edge of the floor he'd been sitting on. Cassie tried to squelch a giggle, but he could see that she was amused by this. "I told you not to wear nice clothes on site."

Lesson learned. He hoped at least the tear wouldn't expose too much of him.

CHAPTER FOUR

WHILE CASSIE AND the brothers finished demolishing the house, John focused his attention on the design. He'd need solid ideas before Monday, so he immersed himself in homes. Books. Magazines. House renovation programs on television. He started a vision board online, posting ideas into a folder that soon grew so large he couldn't remember if he'd already saved something.

When staying in his apartment got too much and everything started to look the same, he signed up for a seminar at a Detroit Public Library branch on the Art Deco movement and its influence on architecture and home design. Not that it matched what he wanted to do in their house, but it could inspire other ideas.

The Thursday-afternoon crowd at the library's auditorium consisted mostly of senior citizens, along with a handful of college-age students who sat near the front row with notebooks and tablets poised for the lecture. John took a seat about halfway down the aisle and checked his phone for any last messages before powering it off.

"John?"

He didn't have to look at the face to recognize that voice. Inwardly cringing, he raised his eyes to find his ex-fiancée standing in the aisle. "Alison." He stood, his mother's training reminding him that he was always a gentleman, despite the circumstances. "How are you?"

"Great." She seemed to be judging his appearance, starting from his shoes and moving her way up. "And you?"

He didn't answer immediately, unsure of what to say. *Lonely since you left. Angry that you broke things off. Relieved that I found out since what kind of person you were before we got married.* But he kept all that to himself and replied, "Fine. I didn't know you were into Art Deco. Modern was more your style."

"I took the day off from work for some me time. This seemed a better option than more shopping." She crossed her arms over her chest. "I saw you in the newspaper recently. You're now an interior decorator? Really, John, I'm surprised at you."

He bristled at her comments and tried to keep an even tone. "It's home design, first of all. And surprised at what, exactly? That I took a chance on a new career, or that someone actually realized that I have talent beyond cars?"

"That you'd sell yourself out for some contest."

His face turned warm and his heart rate sped up. "This is about more than just a contest, Ali. It's about reinventing myself."

"But to be paired with that criminal's daughter?" She shook her head, the sleek blond bun on top of her head bobbing. "I guess I expected more of you."

"You wouldn't have left me if you had. You gave up on me long before this." He glanced behind her. "Isn't your newest acquisition here with you? He's what? A lawyer or doctor? I heard you had traded up. Isn't that the phrase you used?"

Her mouth tightened in a frown. "I thought we could be civil after all this time."

It had been a year and a half. And she was the one who had left him blindsided, with little explanation but a whole lot of put-downs, like she was doing now. He didn't feel the need to be friendly any longer. "As always, Alison, you thought wrong."

Her mouth opened and then snapped shut, as if she were outraged yet speechless. She continued up the aisle to take a seat.

John knew there had been a chance that they would cross paths one day, but admittedly, he'd hoped that he would be coming off his latest triumph instead of starting his newest challenge. Still, what had he seen in Alison beyond the sleek exterior? At the moment, he came up with a very short list of admirable qualities. Thoughts of Cassie intruded, and he smiled. He wondered what she would have told Alison. Though she might not admit it, Cassie was a spitfire, unafraid to speak the truth. Underneath her casual T-shirts and jeans beat the heart of a woman who didn't give up when things got tough.

He settled into his seat as the lecturer stood at the podium. Yes, coming to the seminar had been a great idea.

MUSCLES SHE DIDN'T remember having ached as Cassie entered Lucille's Pizzeria to pick up dinner. The smell of garlic and cheese invited her inside as she pushed open the door. Sal, Lucille's husband, was at the register and waved to her before handing change to the customer in front of him.

Although she didn't need to read the menu, since she'd heard it hadn't changed in the forty-plus years Lucille had been in business, Cassie perused the items before deciding on her usual. Waiting for Sal to finish with his customer, she glanced around the tiny front of the restaurant. Sal had wanted to expand the business to include those who preferred to dine in, but he'd been outvoted by his wife. Lucille insisted that you didn't mess with success.

The customer left, and Cassie edged forward. "Hey, Sal. I'll take the usual."

"Large deep dish with double olives. Got it." He wrote it on a slip and passed it through the window to the kitchen area. "You know, we've got a new app so that you can order ahead of time and it's ready when you arrive."

Since when had Lucille agreed to come

into the twenty-first century? Probably one of her sons had convinced her. Still, nothing beat walking in and ordering her dinner with Sal. "But then we wouldn't get a chance to chat."

Sal chuckled and wiped down the counter with a damp cloth. "Heard you made it into that contest."

"You saw that?"

"Everyone from the neighborhood is talking about it." He paused and leaned on the counter. "You sure make us proud, girl."

She huffed out a long breath. "Don't get too ahead of yourself. I still have a long way to go to win this contest."

"But you are going to win and show those other fellows a thing or two."

She kissed her fingertips and raised her hand to the ceiling. "Let's hope you're right."

"Is that Cassie out there?" Lucille, a large woman in a pristine white apron, walked out of the kitchen and came around the counter to hug her. "I saw that double olive order and knew it had to be you. How are you doing?"

She wasn't sure how to answer. Demolition would be finished the next morning if she had anything to say about it. And then the real work would begin. "Keeping busy, as always."

"You going to show those other contractors who's the boss?"

"That's what I told her, Luce."

Lucille smiled and nodded. "Real proud of you for not letting them get to you. For standing up straight and saying, 'Here I am. Judge me for my work. Not for my father.'"

"But he's still the first thing they think of when they see my name. It's hard to get out from under his shadow." And hard to accept that these two people on the perimeter of her life said the words she'd longed to hear from Daddy.

Sal joined Lucille, putting an arm around his wife's waist. "You're not under his shadow, love. The only one who thinks that is you. It's time for you to be on your own."

"And what if I can't do it by myself?" This is what kept her awake at night. What if after all this she tried and failed? What if her success in the past had been her father all along, and not her own merits? She shook off their protests. "I know that I'm being hard on myself. But when have you known me not to be?"

Sal put his arms on her shoulders and kissed both her cheeks. "We've watched you grow from a little snot-nosed kid who only ate cheese pizza to the fine young woman you are, double olives and all. You may not be blood, but you're family all the same." They caught up on neighborhood business for several more minutes.

"Double olive pizza up," someone shouted from the back, and a box of pizza slid through the window.

Cassie started to dig for her wallet, but Lucille waved her off. "Your money is no good here tonight, hon. But you listen to a piece of advice from Lucille. You're only as good as you think you are." She tapped Cassie on the shoulders. "You chew on that while you eat dinner."

Cassie pulled out a $10 bill and stuffed it into the front pocket of Lucille's apron. When the older woman protested, Cassie insisted. "For the advice."

Cassie ruminated on what Lucille had

said as she drove home and then guided Evie into the backyard. Inside the house, she placed the box of pizza on the kitchen counter and found a paper plate for her first slice. She pulled out a longneck beer from the refrigerator and claimed a seat at the card table by the window to eat dinner.

Outside, Evie chased a squirrel up a tree and barked up at it as it chattered back at her. Cassie smiled at the dog's antics, knowing that Evie didn't understand that the squirrel didn't see her as a friend. All the squirrel could see was a big dog with big teeth and a loud bark.

What did Cassie see when she looked at her possibilities? She was probably more like the squirrel than she'd care to admit. The future that loomed before her looked just as scary, with big teeth and a loud bark, waiting to tear her apart. Okay, so she was being overly dramatic. But she was the type that saw the glass as empty rather than one that could be refilled.

As she ate her pizza, she thought over what Lucille had said. Her entire life had been spent with Daddy's voice in her ears. If she brought home a B from school, why wasn't it an A? If she retiled a bathroom, why hadn't she done it faster?

What would it have cost her father to say he was proud of her? Proud of what she had done?

Her work for him had been scrutinized under the microscope of how it reflected on him. Her ideas and effort claimed by him. And she'd let him because he was her father and the owner of the company. Now that he wasn't here, it fell on her shoulders. And what if it wasn't good enough?

WITH DEMOLITION FINISHED by the first week, it was time for John to finalize the design ideas since they would determine the floor plan and flow of the layout. He invited Cassie and the Buttucci brothers after work Saturday night for dessert and coffee at his apartment to present his vision to the team. He glanced around the living room at the twenty-inch square foam boards he'd used to pin the design elements, including swatches of color and fabric. He hoped Cassie would approve.

A buzz at the intercom by the front door

told him that his first guest had arrived. He pressed the button to speak. "Cassie?"

"Yep, it's me."

"I'm on the fourth floor. Four-o-eight."

He pressed another button to unlock the front door of the apartment building, then waited a few minutes for her to make it to his floor. A soft knock on his door, and he opened it to find her standing alone. He looked behind her, but the hallway was empty. "No brothers tonight?"

"They're tired. I told them to go home."

He'd hoped for their input, but he could understand her concern for the guys. She passed by him, and he could smell the fresh floral scent of her shampoo. She must have showered before coming over. She walked to the first foam board, arms akimbo, and frowned at the design. He stepped in front of her to block her view. "You can see it all after dessert."

She eyed him as if ready to argue but then acquiesced with a nod. He led her into the dining room, where he had set the apple pie, four plates and forks. "I've got ice cream if you'd like it à la mode."

She took a seat in one of the chairs. "It's

been a long day, and I'd rather get this finished and go home to my bed."

He put a piece of pie on a plate and handed it to her with a fork and spoon. "Coffee's brewing. Just sugar, right?"

"Thanks." She took a bite of the pie and moaned. "Is that caramel in the sauce? I'm dying."

He placed the coffee in front of her. "I'm glad you like it. It's my mom's own recipe."

She paused in her chewing and peered at the pie. After she swallowed, she asked, "You made this yourself?"

"You know I don't cook. But I did ask my mom to make it for our evening." He placed a slice of pie on his own plate and joined her at the table.

"If you want to bring one of these to the work site, I wouldn't turn it away."

He chuckled, and they ate in companionable silence. He pointed at her with his fork. "I know you're not sold on the salvaging idea for the design yet, but by the end of the night you'll be convinced."

She paused in her eating and considered his words. "It's not that I don't like the idea, but I'm not confident it's one that can win us the contest. Everything we do has to be top-notch. No room for error."

"It will be. You'll see."

"I'm not sure that's a gamble we should take."

"So we play it safe and make our house look like what everyone else is doing?" He shook his head and played with his fork. "That won't win us any points, either."

"Maybe."

He grinned and put another piece of pie on her plate. "Admit it. I'm right."

She held up her hand. "Enough pie. I want to see what you came up with."

He gave her the plate and ushered her into the living room where she sat on the sofa and continued eating. He stood next to the layout for the kitchen. "Two things about houses usually win people over— kitchens and bathrooms. I figured we'd focus most of our attention and wow factor on these two rooms."

"The judges are going to be looking at the whole house."

"I understand, but this would give us a chance for more impact. With the entire kitchen being gutted before we took possession, we got a blank slate. I'd like to open the wall adjoining the living room."

"Bad news. That's a support wall."

"Yes, but we can put in a window that would give us sight lines into the living room and make it look more spacious. That also leaves us places for cabinets for storage." He pointed to the wood chip he'd picked up from the home improvement store. "Lighter colors will make things look more open as well. But not white, which shows dirt and grime, especially if a young family is chosen for us."

"And the yellow paint chip there?"

"It will make things look warm and inviting, taking advantage of the light coming from all the windows facing the backyard. And we'll pair that yellow with some blues and greens to keep it from being too harsh." He pointed to the floor plan. "We'll keep the sink where the original was, but use that salvaged deep sink that is narrower to maximize counter space. Dishwasher adjacent."

She stood and approached the design. "The placement of the stove and refrigerator won't work like this. You want them to be set up in a triangle with the sink." She found a pencil and marred his layout by changing the location of the stove. "You've got it way over here, but if we move it here. Or even better..." She drew a rectangle in the middle of the kitchen. "On an island and move the refrigerator on this wall." She connected the sink, refrigerator and stove with lines. "See? A triangle."

He took the pencil from her. "And if we add this island with the stove, we can add more storage and a pot holder above." He sketched his idea, then stood back and nodded. "I see what you're saying."

"The kitchen and dining room is the biggest area of our house, so we can add an island without sacrificing much space. And like you said, we gain some storage."

"And we can get a built-in microwave and add it here to free up some counter space, as well." He drew in his idea.

Cassie took the pencil from him and added a seating area on the end of the island. "For more casual dining. And I'll add a lazy Susan in the cabinet here so it's easier access since we don't have the room to add a pantry."

"I like it."

"So do I." She looked up at him. "What else do you have for me?"

FOR THE NEXT HOUR, they went over each of the designs and made changes and improvements. Cassie enjoyed the back-and-forth they had established. John was willing to listen to her about the practicality of a design based on her experience, and she could concede some design ideas because of his vision for the house. He'd even been able to incorporate the high-tech gadgets into the design for maximum impact.

The only thing he wouldn't give up was his idea of using salvaged materials, and she still wasn't sold on it. Even when he showed her how he'd use one of the doors they'd removed earlier that week to create a headboard for the bed in the master bedroom. She wrinkled her nose. "I don't know. Besides the fact that it's a door, you're talking about drilling it to the wall. What if the new owner doesn't like it where you've put it?"

"Trust me."

She eyed him, remembering their conversation the other day. Still, he had some good ideas. "We're more than a month away from being at that point, so we can revisit it then."

"I know what I'm talking about."

"I don't doubt that, but we want to make things look beautiful and be practical. When you're talking about small spaces, you need more flexibility."

He furrowed his brow as he turned back to the design. "I'll see what I can do. Make things more movable. But I'm using the door."

Cassie yawned and took a seat on the sofa. "I think you're going in the right direction, so we'll start bright and early on Monday morning. I'll be working on the initial plumbing while the brothers check the electrical wiring."

"And me?"

She hesitated. "Based on your drawings, you have items you need to build. Whether you do that at the house or somewhere else is up to you."

"You don't want me there."

She didn't want him in the way, but she couldn't just blurt that out. "You did say that you had wired your own sound system, so you can focus on the gadgets. Speaking of, do you have other ideas in your own place?"

"Are you asking for a tour?"

She stood and nodded. "I need to get an idea of your aesthetic."

"I'm making it up as I go, Cassie. This is new for me."

"But you've decorated your own home. Show me that, and I can get a sense of your personal style. Your likes and dislikes."

He didn't seem convinced but led her down the hall nonetheless. She'd expected a guy's bathroom: basic and functional. Instead, he had painted the walls a soft gray and paired it with navy blue towels and a fluffy white bath rug. His accessories were plated nickel. The effect gave the entire room a cool, calm feeling. "I like this."

He ushered her to what was his office. A large drawing easel took up most of the room, and he'd left the walls painted white. However, the effect wasn't stark since he had placed colorful drawings around the room. Some of them were cars, which she had expected, but others surprised her. She walked to a painting of a woman holding a mug and staring out a window. Feeling the woman's loneliness, she touched one of the brushstrokes. "This is amazing. Who's the artist?"

"John Robison."

"I didn't realize that you painted like this."

"It's just one painting, Cass."

She motioned with her hand to the room. "This is all you, right?" She took a step closer to the painting of the woman. "Who was she?"

"No one." John tucked his hands into this pockets and looked away.

"I'm guessing an ex-girlfriend, then."

John shook his head. "No. Are we done with the tour?"

She moved past him out of the room and started toward the closed door at the end of the hallway. He stepped in front of her. "Tour's over, Cassie."

"I haven't seen your bedroom yet. What's the big deal? You hiding a dead body in there?"

"No one goes into my bedroom without an invitation. And I didn't invite you in."

"I'm not asking to move in. Just to get a peek."

"This is my private space. My personal sanctuary." He positioned himself so that she couldn't get her hand on the doorknob.

She feinted to the right, but he seemed to expect her attempt to fake him out and brought her up against him. She looked up at him and found herself eye level with his mouth. He had nice lips, full and inviting. She tipped her head up to see him smirking at her, which only irritated her.

So she kissed him.

He responded, but only for seconds before he stepped back. Using his shock to her advantage, she squeezed under his arms to open the door. But once the doorknob turned and the door cracked open, she knew she'd done the wrong thing. Without saying a word, he pointed at her to return to the living room, where she slumped on the sofa.

"Sorry."

His lips were pursed angrily. "There are lines you can't cross if we're going to make this partnership work, Cassie."

"I only wanted to see your bedroom."

Man, she sounded pathetic and whiny. She felt like she was four years old and being called on the carpet for her misdeeds. She hung her head. "Sorry."

"You said we have to build trust between us. And I agree. But you're playing games with me, and I don't like it."

She nodded. "You're right. I shouldn't have kissed you." She stood and pulled her keys out of her jeans pocket. "I'll say good-night now."

Before she reached the door, John called out her name. "Wait." He joined her. "I'll walk you to your truck."

"I'll be fine."

"I'd feel better knowing you got to your car safely."

He opened the door to let her walk out first. He pulled a set of keys from a copper bowl on a table by the entry and followed her downstairs. They were silent as they walked to her truck. She kept her eyes straight ahead, except for when she snuck a glance at him and noticed the splotches of red on his neck and cheeks.

"I am sorry, John. I shouldn't have taken advantage of you like that."

He gave a short nod, then tapped the roof of her vehicle before turning and walking back to his building. She slipped into her truck and watched his retreat in the rear-view mirror. "You messed up, Cass. Big time," she told herself.

It wasn't just the kiss, and she knew it. She had tried to enter where she wasn't wanted, forced herself into his personal space. How many times had that happened to her? Swallowing her regret, she put the truck into gear and drove home.

EVEN WITH A long list of things to do, they had decided to wait until Tuesday, after the Memorial Day long weekend, to start fixing up the house. But that didn't mean John couldn't stop by and walk through to make more notes. He wanted to get a feel of the place without the entire team there and figured that this might be his last chance for solitude.

He stared at the brick exterior, thinking about what he knew. Loretta had mentioned that the Czarnecks had once lived here. What had happened to them? Did they have happy memories here? Bittersweet? Had there been more laughter or tears inside its walls? He hoped it was the former. People didn't laugh enough these days.

The door creaked as he opened it and stepped inside the house. It still smelled dusty from all the plaster they had removed, as well as the sawdust from cutting out rotten floorboards. Skirting the hole in the living room, he walked into the kitchen and put a hand on the doorjamb. Had the kids lined up to have their heights measured with pencil marks? Were gourmet masterpieces created in this kitchen or were meals a hodgepodge of this and that?

The unknown history of the home seemed to distract him from what he'd been pondering since Saturday night. Why had he enjoyed Cassie kissing him? Even after he realized she'd used the kiss to get past him into his bedroom, he still wanted to keep kissing her. It had been a shock when her lips had touched his, but it had been welcome all the same. His anger had been at her betrayal of his trust rather than the kiss. He hadn't been able to talk much as he ushered her out to her truck. Could barely keep his emotions in check.

He shook his head. The worst thing would be to get involved with her while they renovated the house. He wanted... No, he *needed* to keep their relationship on a professional level. He couldn't let his own desires for her distract him from his job. He had to lock up his heart for the next few months while they worked. Keep his eyes focused on the design, not how cute she was when she got excited about their project. The way her bourbon-colored eyes crinkled in the corners when she smiled. Her eager enthusiasm made him only want her more.

Stop. Thinking. About. Her.

He glanced around the empty space and decided he needed to do something to bring his focus back. He knew his designs lacked that something special, even after Cassie had drawn her own ideas on them. Together, they had come up with some better strategies but he knew he was missing that one thing that would take them over the top. Maybe a walk would clear his head.

Curiosity got the better of him and he

strolled past the other contest homes. One of the teams had decided to work on the holiday if the sounds of hammers and saws were any indication. He wondered how they were handling the design concept, but he didn't need the ideas of others to cloud his focus. He had enough confidence in his own skills to not have to take from anyone else.

As he got closer to the busy street, the smells of charcoal and grilled meat filled the air. He sniffed appreciatively. He'd declined his mother's invitation to accompany her to her family reunion in Missouri because of the contest deadline. He needed to be thinking about the house, instead of chatting with cousins he hadn't seen in years. He'd also turned down his friend Brett's invite to join him and his family at their cottage up north. This left him alone for the holiday.

He crossed the street and saw Loretta rocking on her porch. She shaded her eyes and called out to him, "John, you working today?"

"No, ma'am. I wanted to go look at the

house to get some inspiration before we start work tomorrow."

She nodded as she fanned herself. "I found some pictures that I thought you might like." She grunted as she stood. "Now where did I leave them?" She turned back to look at him. "Well, don't just stand there. Come in and help me find them."

He couldn't help but notice the bustle of activity inside the house, especially the kitchen. A woman smiled at him after Loretta introduced him. "You were right, Mama. John stopped by."

"I told you he would."

"I'm her daughter, Shekinah. Mama hasn't stopped talking about you. You staying for barbecue?"

"No, I couldn't."

Loretta looked at him knowingly. "You have other plans?"

"No, ma'am."

"Then you're staying." She said it as if there was no doubt. "Now, where did I put those pictures for John?"

"On the front table by your chair so you wouldn't forget." Her daughter reminded her. "Can I get you something to drink, John? Water? Pop? Iced tea?"

"Thank you. Tea sounds great."

Loretta shook her head. "Don't grow old. You lose your memory. Your body." She sighed and walked back to the living room where she found the pictures stacked on a side table. "The Czarnecks were known for their elaborate Christmas parties. I thought you might like to see how the house used to be."

He took the glossy pictures and started to flip through them. "These are fantastic. Thank you." He peered at one photo of the kitchen. Six adults sat at a table by the bay window. "They used the window seat for a table. That was my plan, too."

"The adults used to crowd in there and play cards while the kids ran about and had their own games." She smiled, re-membering. "And Layla could cook like a dream. She was known for her chicken-and-rice casserole." Loretta smacked her lips. "Those were the days we didn't worry about too much butter or cheese."

John looked at the pictures. There was one of the living room with a tall Christmas tree at the large window. Four kids crowded on a sofa, holding gifts and smiling with quite a few missing teeth among them. Another of a woman being kissed on the cheek by a man hiding a bouquet of flowers behind his back. John held the picture up to Loretta. "Were they the Czarnecks?"

Loretta took the photo from him and peered at it. "Yes, that's Layla and Tom. My, he loved that woman. Thought she could do no wrong."

"What happened to them?"

She thrust the picture at him. "Their oldest boy got killed in a car accident. Only sixteen. It affected Layla so. She let her grief eat her up until Tom moved the family down South somewhere. He thought that a move might bring her out of her depression."

"Did it?"

"Seemed to. We exchanged Christmas cards for a while, but eventually that stopped." Loretta sighed. "Sometimes it's hard to remember the neighborhood we once had. Block parties with enough food to feed a couple neighborhoods. The kids would play tag and ride their bikes until they had to come inside for bed. And there was a community garden." She sat forward and stared at him. "Did I tell you about the garden?"

"No, ma'am."

She leaned back in her recliner. "It was hard trying to raise a family on one income in those days, so someone got this idea that we should grow some of our own food. We each had our own small gardens, but we needed additional space to expand. There was an empty lot, so we tilled it and planted a bunch of vegetables. Ears of corn by the bushel. The best tomatoes I ever ate. And enough green beans that we canned for days and it fed us through the winter."

Shekinah handed John a glass of iced tea. "Is she telling you about the garden? I remember the strawberries we planted one year. I would pick a handful, wash 'em and eat 'em right away."

"I'd forgotten the strawberries." Loretta smacked her lips. "We ate strawberry short-cake for dessert practically every night for a month. You know, I heard that community gardens are back in style these days. Wish we could start one again here."

"Where would we put it, Mama? There's no empty lots on this street anymore."

"I know, I know. Just wishful thinking, I guess." She looked out the window to the front yard. "And I don't have the energy to plant my own."

John had never planted a garden, not even as a child. After his parents divorced when he was seven, he'd grown up in apartment buildings and condos without backyards. There'd been no room for growing his own food, or anything else for that matter. Hearing them talk about the bounty they'd harvested from the community garden stirred a longing in him that he'd never known. Maybe they should plant a garden in the backyard of the house. Not just flowers, but tomatoes, corn and green beans like Loretta suggested.

But then, what did he know about growing a garden?

A tall man entered the living room carrying several bags of food. "The party has arrived." He frowned at John. "You made a new friend, Ma?"

Shekinah took the bags from the man as Loretta stood and motioned to John. "This is John. He's working on one of the contest houses down the street. John, this is my son, Walter Junior."

"Call me Junie."

"Pleasure to meet you."

The two men shook hands as the front door opened again and more people filtered into the house. Loretta introduced John to them all and he made an effort to remember their names. There had to have been at least twenty new arrivals. When Shekinah announced that the food was ready, they moved en masse to the backyard, where card tables and lawn chairs had been set up. John found Loretta. "I really should go. I don't want to horn in on your family picnic."

"Nonsense. There's more than enough to eat, so you're staying." She pointed to the man at the charcoal grill. "Besides, you never had my husband Walter's ribs. He's won awards for them."

Seeing that he didn't have much choice, he joined the group moving down the buffet line. Someone thrust a paper plate at him, and he ogled the variety of choices. He vaguely remembered going with his mother to a family Christmas party where a huge spread had been provided for dinner, but Loretta's family seemed to have made every kind of summer dish. He helped himself to a little of each and ended at the grill where Walter Sr. placed a half slab of ribs on top of everything. "Thank you for joining us today, son."

"Thank you for inviting me."

After everyone had eaten too much, Shekinah and Loretta brought out several desserts despite protests that they were all full. John looked around the backyard as the younger members of the family stacked cookies in their hands before sitting in the shade of the garage. Loretta brought over a small bowl of strawberry shortcake and placed it in front of him before sitting in the empty chair next to his. "Did you get enough to eat?"

John laughed and patted his belly. "I don't think I could eat a bite of those strawberries." When she started to take it away, he stopped her. "But I'll give it a try."

"I like to see someone with a good appetite. You're welcome to join us for the Fourth if you don't have plans."

"You have a wonderful family, Miss Loretta. I'm jealous. It's been just my mom and me for so long."

"No brothers or sisters?"

He shook his head. "I did always want a brother, but it never happened."

"And your father?"

"He divorced my mom, and I saw him for two weeks every summer for a while until even that didn't happen." He'd long ago given up on the idea of having a relationship with his dad. He had his mom and he was grateful for that. "I don't think he wanted children. I seemed to be an inconvenience to him."

"Well, you seem like a nice young man, so he missed out."

"Thank you for that." He ate a bite of the shortcake and closed his eyes in appreciation. "Is this real whipped cream?"

Loretta gave him a smile. "That's the problem with you kids today. You're used to the fake stuff that comes in the can."

"I'm hardly a kid."

"You are to me."

John grinned and continued to eat his strawberry shortcake as Loretta continued speaking, "I'm not saying that everything in those days was perfect. You know, it's too bad you can't take the great things from the past and combine them with the good stuff now."

John paused eating and put his spoon down. "Say that again?"

Loretta sighed. "I just think if we could combine what we loved about the good old days with what we enjoy now, life would be pretty near perfect. Trouble is, we're likely to tear down the old to make way for the new. Couldn't we combine them both?"

Images of the house started to fill his head. Combining the old with the new. Using what was best about the past with the technological innovations of today. He nodded. It could work. But that would mean changing the designs. Again.

Although this could be the idea that would help them win.

CASSIE SAT ON the chaise on the patio in her parents' backyard and flipped through the pages of a magazine. Her mother watered the flowers. If they were selling the house, she wasn't sure why her mom was making the effort. Granted, she knew about curb appeal when it came to selling a house, but her mother seemed to be going overboard.

Her mother wound the hose after she was finished and joined Cassie on the patio. "Are you disappointed we didn't barbecue this year?"

"Daddy was the one who manned the grill. Didn't seem like any point."

Her mother nodded and they fell silent. Cassie pretended to be reading an article, but she couldn't focus on the words. Instead, she wondered where her father was. Had he left the country? Canada was only across the river, so maybe he had fled there. "Do you think he's okay?"

"I think he believes he's better off there than here."

Cassie peered at her mother. "Do you really think he did it?"

Her mother blinked but kept her gaze steady on her. "The evidence is pretty overwhelming that he did, sweetheart. I know that you don't want to believe that he'd betray us like that, but…"

"Because he wouldn't."

Her mother came to sit next to her on the chaise, putting a hand on hers. "But he did."

"Why would he steal from his own company? It doesn't make sense to me."

"Maybe if he ever calls you again, you can ask him that."

"He only called the one time, Mother."

"Good."

Cassie removed her hand from her mother's. "I miss him. And I can't run the company without him."

Her mother stood and looked down on her. "Cassandra, there is no company anymore. We've sold most of the assets to pay back what your father took, and that means Lowman Construction is done."

"But…" Weren't there other ways to pay back the money? If they sold the company, what would she do? What was the point of entering the contest to win the prize money to keep the company going if Lowman Construction was already gone? She tilted her head back and closed her eyes. The Belvedere Foundation was paying her a stipend while she worked on the contest house, but that would end once the judging took place. "What will I do then?"

"What do you mean, dear?"

"That was my future."

"So you'll come up with another one."

Cassie's heart sank. Did her mother really think she could just conjure up another plan for her life? Since she had turned twelve and started working onsite with her dad, she'd been anticipating taking over for him when he eventually retired. There was nothing else for her.

Her cell phone buzzed in her shorts pocket, and she pulled it out and swiped the bar to answer it. "Hello?"

"Hey, it's John. Am I interrupting anything?"

Only her life falling apart. Cassie stood and walked away to find a little privacy. She hadn't expected to hear from him after the other night. They had to work together, which meant her kissing him had been the wrong impulse to follow. She took a deep breath. "About the other night…"

"Don't worry about it. It's forgotten."

Okay. Maybe it was better to do that so they could keep their relationship on a professional basis. "Is something wrong?"

A long pause. "I'm changing the designs."

"What? No, we start tomorrow. It's too late to change gears."

"But we haven't finalized the materials yet or paid for them. And I think you'll like this new direction."

She rubbed her forehead with her free hand. "John, we agreed to the plans the other night. That's what we're sticking with."

"Just let me show you the new sketches. I'm sure you'll agree with what I've come up with."

"And what is that?"

"I've got pictures of what the house used to look like. I can bring some of those elements into the new look. Sort of retro meets high tech."

She considered his words and his burst of enthusiasm, and had to admit that the direction intrigued her. Maybe that was the idea that would put them over the top compared to the other teams.

And now that there was no company to save, all she had was winning this contest so she could create that new future for herself.

CHAPTER FIVE

JOHN PULLED UP to the house the next morning. He hadn't felt this excited about his work in a long time.

He brought the new designs with him into the house and propped them against a wall in the kitchen. Eyeing a box of doughnuts, he chose a cruller and moaned. Sugar and caffeine would get him through the day. Fresh-brewed coffee was in the pot and he poured himself a cup.

Cassie flipped through the designs as he finished his doughnut and drank his coffee. "You worked on these since we talked?"

"I told you I would."

"But you only had a few hours, realistically." He stood behind her as she studied the changes. When she finally finished looking at the last board, she went back to the first and started the process over. The suspense was killing him. Did she like them? Hate them? He couldn't tell by her body language.

After she finished her second pass, she looked over her shoulder at him and he could see a gleam in her whiskey-brown eyes. "You're right," she said. "These are better."

He wanted to pump his fist in the air but kept his expression neutral. "Thanks."

"I've been thinking about something you said a couple weeks ago. About wanting to see the original blueprints." She tapped her lips with her finger. "We could go to city hall and ask if they have copies on file, but I wonder if we'd have some luck in the attic. Builders often stored copies there."

The attic with the creepy crawlies? He shivered. "Do we really have to go up there?"

She nodded and laid a hand on his bare arm. "Don't worry. I'll protect you from the spiders."

He swallowed hard and told himself that she was teasing. But still, as he climbed the ladder to go through the hatch to the attic, he repeated to himself that he was much bigger than any spider they might find.

What they found in the attic surprised him. He'd expected it to be emptied by the previous owners. Instead, there was furniture, boxes and a large trunk. The room was filled to the rafters. Cassie stepped around the trunk, and as he boosted himself up, his foot hooked on the top rung, knocking the ladder to the floor below. He grimaced at it, then turned to find Cassie staring at him with an open mouth.

"I'm pretty tall. Maybe I can let myself down and drop the last few feet. Then you could use the ladder."

She seemed to hide a smile and said, "We'll figure it out later." They started to survey the myriad of stuff that crowded the attic. "Careful. Some of these joists are rotten. I don't want you to take the wrong step and fall through the floor."

Taking her advice, he tiptoed to an old metal pedal car. "I haven't seen one of these in years. There's not many still around." He squatted beside it and ran a hand along its rusted exterior. "I wonder if the Czarnecks left it here."

Cassie began to open boxes. "There's china. Old clothes. A whole bunch of books by authors I've never heard of. Why would they leave all of this?"

"Maybe they forgot about it. Or they figured there was nothing worth keeping." He opened a box and pulled out some papers. "We might find the plans in this one. It looks like paperwork. Maybe from the original sale."

Cassie joined him and together they sifted through the various documents. She took a seat next to the box and perused several pages. "Tax information. Mortgage information. They really didn't want to take this with them?"

"They were trying to escape their grief." When Cassie stared at him, he explained, "I talked to Miss Loretta about the family and found out they moved after their oldest son was killed."

"She's a wealth of information."

He agreed and then gave a cry of triumph as he pulled out a haphazardly folded sheaf. "Floor plans, I'll bet."

He spread the large paper across the floor. Cassie pointed to where the mudroom now existed. "They had an option for a basement. Wonder why they decided to go with a crawl space instead."

John sat back on his heels. "To keep costs down, perhaps. If all these houses were built with similar plans by the same builder, they might have been trying to build more with less money."

"Sounds about right." She started to smile. "We're above the living room right now. If we took down the ceiling to open up the room, we could really make a visual impact when the judges come into the house."

"Take down the ceiling?"

She nodded. "We might be sacrificing the storage space in the attic, but from the looks of things up here, we'd have to finish off the floors so things didn't fall through below. Instead, we open up the living room and kitchen with vaulted ceilings." She stood and wiped her hands off on her shorts. "We won't be like everybody else's design that way. We'll truly have a unique concept."

"More demo?" he asked, unsure of how he felt about this.

Smiling, she put her hands on her hips. "There's nothing better."

AFTER REMOVING THE items from the attic and storing them in the garage to look through later, the Buttucci brothers got to knocking down the ceiling. Biggie especially seemed to be enjoying the process. His smile stretched from ear to ear.

With the ceiling in the living room and kitchen removed, Tiny stared up at the open space. "We'll need to reinforce the joists before we add insulation and drywall."

Cassie added those to the list of things they would need to buy for this next phase of construction. "Did John go home already?"

"In the garage. He has an idea for a tile mosaic and wanted to go through those boxes of china we found in the attic."

He was certainly fixated on using old items. But like he said, if they could marry the past with the future in their designs, it could potentially give them an advantage over the competition. She ripped the page with the list of needed supplies off her notebook and handed it to Tiny. "If you and your brother could go get these items, I'll take John with me to the architectural salvage yard that he suggested. We might be able to find some things there."

"I've never built with junk, Cass."

"And we won't start now." She put a hand on his shoulder. "But maybe he's right. Things were made to last when this house was built. We could probably find quality fixtures that won't need to be replaced every five to ten years."

He didn't look convinced. She wasn't sure she was completely on board with this idea, either, but they had to give it a try.

The salvage setup was unlike anything Cassie had ever seen before. It was less of a store and more of a warehouse that housed everything from fixtures to lumber, tiling to appliances. She ran her hand along hard pine flooring. She loved the golden look of the wood and wondered where they could use it in the house. There was only a small amount. It didn't look like enough to replace the floor in the living room.

John walked up to her. "That would work great in the master bedroom."

Of course. She should have seen it herself.

"Come on over here. I want to show you something."

She followed him outside to an area that seemed to be full of items intended for the trash pile. John pulled out a stainless steel sink that was rusted in spots. It was deep but narrow, much like what he had wanted for the kitchen. "Isn't it great?"

"It's full of rust."

"It's only on the surface. It hasn't eaten through the steel, so it can be scoured to look like new."

She wasn't convinced yet. "Why are we buying junk?"

"It's not junk. It just needs a little extra love and care." He held it up and inspected it more carefully. "This looks like it will outlive us both. And you know we'll be able to get a great discount on it."

She winced and scanned the outdoor area. "Let's find a cart to put it in while we keep looking."

John smiled as if he'd won the argument and carried the sink inside the warehouse. She moved along the rows of discarded light fixtures. Most of them looked as if they belonged in a different century and would be out of place in their house. But then a glint of green caught her eye, and she pulled a stained glass shade off one of the shelves. In triangles of varying hues of blues and greens, the design reminded her of a Tiffany lamp. But this was made to hang from the ceiling, likely over a table. In her mind's eye, she could see it hanging over the kitchen table at the window seat.

She heard John coming up the aisle with the cart and held up the light fixture. "Tell me where you see this."

"Above the kitchen table."

She nodded and smiled as she placed it on the flat pallet cart with the sink. Okay, so maybe this salvage idea wasn't a horrible one. Maybe they could marry the past with the future in the designs of their house. "We still need cabinets, more light fixtures, flooring, counters…"

John stood next to a metal table and put his hand on the surface. "And a kitchen island."

She scrutinized the piece. "No, looks too industrial for your idea. We need something that has more wood, less steel."

He put the table back. They walked around

and found other items they could use in their house: a pedestal sink that had cracked enamel but could be reglazed, a gooseneck faucet for the kitchen sink with handles that had H and C printed in wavy script, and a matching pair of wall sconces to use in the master bedroom. But no island.

When they checked out with the cashier, Cassie gulped at the total cost. They would have spent twice as much buying new. She had figured that they'd be saving money by going this route, rather than buying all new, but she hadn't understood it would be this much. She paid and tucked the receipt safely in her wallet. At her truck, they put their finds in the bed and headed for a big-box home improvement store.

John wasn't on board with her choice in cabinets and counters for the kitchen, but he agreed to the type of tile for the kitchen and bathroom. They argued over the flooring options for the living room. She wanted to go darker with a maple while he insisted on a lighter choice. Thinking of the pine they'd seen at the salvage store, she agreed to a compromise in a honey-colored oak.

As they stood at the register, waiting to pay, she watched John, who was flipping through an interior design magazine. "Are you determined to fight my choices the entire way?"

He answered but kept his gaze on the magazine. "If, by that, you mean I'm insisting on my design concepts rather than your whims? Yes."

"The maple wasn't a whim. You said you wanted things to have a warm tone, so I pointed out the obvious one."

"Hmm." He pulled out his wallet and paid for the magazine separately. "It seems to me that you believe the only route for us to win is by doing whatever you say."

She winced. It sounded like something she'd accused her father of many times in the past. "I didn't say that."

"Your attitude says it." He glanced at her, then walked to her pickup.

She trailed behind him. "I'm the one with experience fixing up houses, not you. I know what works."

John didn't respond. Instead, he got in the passenger side of the truck and stared straight ahead.

CASSIE DROVE THEM toward the house but first made a detour. He took in the neighborhood street that looked so much like theirs but wasn't. "You made a wrong turn."

"I need to go pick up Evie. I couldn't bring her shopping with us."

So he would get a glimpse of her house. He skimmed over her appearance and wondered if where she lived would be similar to her personal style: practical and down-to-earth. Although she'd been wearing a dress when they first met, he'd only seen her ever since in super casual clothes that were meant for time spent working. Jeans. T-shirts. Steel-toed boots. None of it was bought for their high-end appearance but for what they could withstand. He'd never noticed her wearing any makeup, but she didn't need to. Her big bourbon-colored eyes, the slight slant of her nose and her exquisite cheekbones gave her a beauty that didn't require cosmetics to enhance. She usually kept her chestnut hair in a high ponytail that had its own natural wave.

She parked the truck at a ranch-style house with beige siding that needed to be replaced. He made to follow her. She stopped and asked, "Where are you going? I'll only be a sec."

"I'd like to see your house."

Her eyes narrowed. "Why?"

"Because someone once told me that she wanted to get an idea of my aesthetic by seeing how I designed my home."

She swallowed but didn't soften the tight set of her jaw. "Fine. But I haven't come close to finishing it, so don't expect too much."

The living room had no walls, only wooden studs. No furniture apart from two sawhorses supporting a long trestle on which a rolled blueprint had been left along with an empty coffee mug and several pencils. He wasn't sure what he'd been expecting, but it hadn't been this. "You weren't kidding when you said it wasn't finished."

"I work on it when I have the time, which I had until recently."

Evie barked and started to jump on him. He held out his arms to catch her and rubbed her head. "Is anything finished?"

She motioned him to the back of the house. "I'm inviting you into my bedroom."

Sand-colored carpet. Dark blue walls with a big-screen television. A huge bed took up most of the floor space. It had about a dozen pillows and a cream coverlet. It looked inviting. Soft. She opened a pair of doors that revealed a massive closet that had been specially crafted and very well organized. It held drawers and poles for her clothing as well as shelves for shoes and other personal items. In awe, he turned to her. "You built this?"

"With some of my dad's help before he disappeared."

He stepped forward and touched one of the shelves. "This is fantastic. I didn't realize you did work like this."

"It's not that hard."

He was surprised that she would dismiss such workmanship. "Do you think you could do this at our house? Create a custom closet?"

"Really?" She sounded pleased by his suggestion.

"What homeowner wouldn't want something like this? Maybe we should plan this for all the bedroom closets."

"It's an idea." And just as suddenly, she

had dismissed his praise. He couldn't understand why she didn't have more pride in her own work. She was obviously talented. Couldn't she see that?

"Is this the only room you've finished?"

"It's the one I spend most of my time in when I'm home."

"I can see why."

She cocked an eyebrow and looked him over. "So, now that you've seen my bedroom, will you show me yours?"

He burst out laughing and shook his head. "It's going to take a lot more than that for me to let you in there."

"It was worth a try."

He made to leave the room when he heard her ask softly, "Do you think I can do this?"

He stopped in his tracks and turned back to look at her. She seemed so vulnerable and lost in that moment that it made him ache for her. He wanted to put his arms around her to reassure her that she could do this. That they both could. That not only could they do this, but that they would win this contest and show them all.

But he had the same doubts that she did

and didn't know how to tell her any differently.

Nonetheless, he slipped his hand in hers and held on tight. "We'll both do our best."

JOHN'S MOTHER WALKED slowly and cautiously around the living room of the contest house, careful not to step in the hole in the center of the floor. "Without walls it's hard to tell what this place will look like when it's finished."

"Close your eyes and imagine it though." He did what he'd asked her to do. "Vaulted ceilings. Warm beige walls with white trim. A wall with family pictures. Sofa in front of the picture window."

His mother made a noise of agreement in the back of her throat. "What color sofa?"

"I was thinking white."

"What if your family has children? You want a darker color that can either hide stains or wash them off easily."

He opened his eyes and looked at his mom. "You're right. I need to be more practical in case there's children, especially young ones." Mentally, he changed the sofa from white to navy. No, too dark. Maybe one with a light colored background, but darker florals or even a plaid. "That's why I wanted to bring you here. You have good ideas."

"What about this Cassie? What does she bring to the table?"

John thought of the woman in question and couldn't stop the smile from forming on his lips. "She definitely has strong ideas, but then she's got the experience to back them up. I wish she had a little more confidence in herself, though."

His mother raised an eyebrow at this. "She has strong opinions, but lacks confidence? Those two don't usually go together."

"I think it has to do with her father. From the sounds of things, he either shot down her ideas outright or stole credit for them later on." He'd been learning a lot of about how Cassie's father built houses during his conversations with both her and the Buttucci brothers. Cassie might look up to her father, but John had his doubts about the man.

His mother motioned to the kitchen.

"Tell me what you're going to be doing in here."

He followed her and pointed to the window where they would build a window seat with storage underneath. The island that would house the stove. The double door refrigerator that would take up most of one wall.

His mother nodded in the right places. She had always encouraged him and his goals. After he'd been laid off, she had told him he'd find a new position that would make him happier. When he'd read about the contest in the newspaper, she'd been the first to hear about his plans to apply. She'd supported him through the entire interview process. She always thought he could do whatever he set his mind to.

How different it was to Cassie's experience when she was growing up? She'd share an idea, and her father would shoot it down. No wonder she had doubts about their chances to win the contest. While he had his mother telling him that he couldn't lose, Cassie wondered how they could possibly win.

Maybe he needed to encourage her more.

He turned to find his mother watching him. "Sorry. Got lost in my thoughts there. What did you say?"

His mother gave him a knowing smile. "Thinking of Cassie?"

He stepped closer to his mom and put a hand on her shoulder. "I was thinking that I'm lucky to have you on my side."

"And you're wondering who's on Cassie's."

He nodded. "She's my partner. And I should be behind her and her ideas."

"Sounds like I raised a kind man."

He leaned over and kissed her cheek. "A smart one, too, I hope."

THE FOLLOWING MONDAY MORNING, Cassie discovered the Buttucci brothers sitting on the porch. Something was wrong. She could tell. She parked the truck at the curb and headed up the sidewalk. "What's up?"

Biggie glanced at Tiny, who grimaced. "You don't want to go inside."

"Why wouldn't I?"

"Remember that time that someone vandalized the Carter house we were working on?" Tiny stood and shook his head. "It's not as bad, but it's not pretty."

Cassie brushed past him and all but sprinted into the living room, her jaw dropping and eyes bulging. Someone had used neon orange spray paint to write "Loserz" across the brand-new drywall and filled the hole in the floor with something that smelled like rotten fish. "Wh-why?" she sputtered.

There was shouting from the front yard. "Where is she?"

She followed the noise and found a crowd had gathered on the lawn. Nick pointed at her. "You!"

Biggie stepped in front of her, so she had to peer around his bulky form. "Keep your distance if you know what's good for you."

Different voices came at her from all directions and she took hold of Biggie's arm.

"Why did you sabotage our house?"

"Once a Lowman, always a Lowman."

"Playing the dirty tricks your old man taught you?"

"Stop!" John shouted, coming to stand at the bottom of the porch stairs. "What in the world is going on?"

Nick glared at him. "Trying to protect your girlfriend?"

"I'm trying to figure out what you're talking about. So choose your words carefully and tell me what happened."

"Cassie put an ax through my kitchen countertops!"

"She spray-painted a bunch of cuss words on my garage door!"

"She punched holes in the drywall I was about to hang!"

Cassie stepped around Biggie. "I didn't do any of those things. Our house was sabotaged, same as yours."

John's jaw dropped. "Our house?" He swept past her.

Cassie kept her focus on the crowd gathered below her. "Why would you think that I would damage your houses?"

"Like father, like daughter," Nick raged. "Why wouldn't you sabotage us to give yourself a leg up on the competition?"

It didn't make sense. None of this was making any sense. "And ruin my house at the same time?"

"It would get the attention off you as the guilty party."

John joined her on the porch. "Someone needs to call the police."

Tiny held up his phone. "Already done. They're on their way."

Cassie turned to John. "I didn't do this."

"I know." He put a hand on her arm. "You believe too much in what we're doing to risk it all." To the crowd, he said, "You're pointing your finger at the wrong person."

"Obviously you'd stand up for her." Nick approached them, but Biggie put his arm out to stop his progress. "You can't win this contest through dirty dealings!"

"I'm not dirty, Nick," she shot back.

The man sneered at her. "No one believes you."

That the crowd seemed to agree with him made her heart stutter. Were they going to paint her with the same brush that they'd used to condemn her father, and again, without any evidence? Had she already been counted out of the contest when it had only just started?

A police cruiser drove down the street toward them and stopped in front of Nick's house. Two uniformed officers waded through the crowd as more accusations about her were yelled out. One of the officers put his fingers in his mouth and gave a sharp whistle. Quiet descended, and his partner, a female officer, shouted, "Everyone to their own house. We will interview you one at a time."

When Nick started to protest, she gave him a steely-eyed glare until he nodded and moved along to his house. The group slowly dispersed. John put a hand on her elbow. "Are you okay?" he asked, concern in his eyes.

"Fine. But who would do this?"

"It's probably some kids who think they're being funny." He turned to the Buttucci brothers. "We should probably go inside and wait for the detectives."

Tiny shook his head. "Did you smell how bad it is in there? I don't think I could last five minutes."

"Then maybe we should remove whatever's in that hole."

"I wouldn't recommend it until I've had a chance to photograph it," said the male officer approaching them. "Ben Novakowski, with the Detroit Police. Can you show me what happened to your house?"

John led the way. Cassie could see the officer wince as he took in the sight of what was piles of trash. He pulled his phone out and took pictures of the mess as well as the spray-painted message and other damage. "When was the last time one of you was here?"

"Saturday afternoon," Cassie answered. "We left about four." The Buttucci brothers nodded their agreement.

John held up his finger. "I stopped by yesterday afternoon to take measurements in the bedrooms. I wanted to double-check figures that I had written down earlier in the week."

"What time yesterday?"

"About one." He turned to Cassie. "I had my mom with me. She wanted to see what we were working on."

For some reason, this felt like a betrayal. He'd shown an outsider what they had been doing here? "You showed her the house?"

"It's not exactly a secret."

"My family hasn't stopped by to take a peek." When Biggie cleared his throat behind her, she had to concede. "They probably wouldn't, but still. It's not ready for public eyes."

"Even as the Belvedere Foundation sends

photographers to take pictures for their before and after articles?"

"That's the foundation. Not family."

"Which should make them even more welcome."

The officer held up his hand. "Can we hold off on that argument until after my partner and I are finished here?" He snapped a few more pictures and squeezed his nostrils together. "Let's finish this interview outside."

After Officer Novakowski was satisfied with their answers to his questions, he took his leave and they began the process of removing the trash and opening windows to air out the house. Tiny put a hand to the neon spray paint and shook his head. "Fixing all this damage puts us behind a day."

"It's early. We still have time to catch up." Cassie put a finger through a hole in a sheet of drywall stacked against one wall. "They used a hammer for these holes. What group of kids is hanging out with a hammer?"

"Or an ax to smash through countertops?" John grimaced. "I might have been hasty with that suggestion as to the guilty party. But it made the most sense at the time." His cell phone rang, and he took his call outside.

Cassie addressed the Buttucci brothers. "He's right. The tools those creeps used to damage the houses seem more like what we would use in the construction business."

Tiny positioned an empty bin next to the hole. "You're right, though, about the weapons of choice," he said. "What if one of the contractors who didn't get picked is causing trouble? Maybe a hothead with anger issues."

"You think Bill?" she asked. She thought about how the blustery contractor had said he'd keep an eye on her at the launch event. Maybe he'd taken the threat to the next level and sabotaged their work?

Tiny shrugged. "He once got arrested for hitting an employee with a two-by-four."

"Over twenty years ago, maybe." She shook her head. "He might not like that he didn't get chosen, but he's too busy with his own projects to ruin ours."

"So he couldn't have sent someone to do the job?" Biggie stepped up to the hole.

"Maybe," she admitted. She sighed and

voiced the part that had really hurt. "That was rough having everyone accusing me of this. Let's hope it's a one-time thing," she said.

John returned to the living room and held up his phone to them. "That was Mr. Belvedere. We have a meeting tomorrow morning at the foundation's offices."

Cassie checked her schedule. "That doesn't work for me. There's a delivery I need to be here for and it's happening at nine, so I can't go."

Tiny stepped forward. "I can take care of that, so you can go. No problem."

Another meeting? She was more interested in checking on the flooring delivery and starting to install that. Tiny put a hand on her shoulder as if to reassure her that she could do the meeting. He gave her a wink before leaving the living room to inventory the damage in the kitchen.

Cassie sighed and peered at John. "That solves that problem."

"And what do we do about this?" He gestured to the room.

"Well, the good news is that it's mostly cosmetic." She walked to the wall that had the graffiti painted on it and stared at the word Loserz. The word brought a tear to her eye. "Did I ever tell you what my dad called coming in second place?" She glanced back at John who shook his head. "First loser." She glanced at the graffiti again. "I can't lose, John. I can't."

John walked up behind her and put a hand on her shoulder. She turned into his embrace and held on to him. "You're not a loser, Cassie. Not in any way. Don't ever let some jerk convince you otherwise."

She rested her cheek against his chest, drawing comfort from his kindness.

CHAPTER SIX

THE THOUGHT OF what the directors of the Belvedere Foundation would want to discuss had John tossing and turning for hours that night until he finally fell into a fitful sleep after three. When his alarm woke him at six thirty, he groaned and slapped it off.

Despite his fatigue, he dressed in his running clothes and laced up his sneakers before leaving the apartment for his morning jog. The steady pounding of his feet against the pavement soothed his worried thoughts, and he pushed himself to run faster than usual to keep from thinking. Whatever it was that they had to talk to them about would be okay. He'd survived losing a career he loved. Had borrowed money from his mother until he could get back on his feet. This contest was more than just starting a different direction for him. It meant winning money that he could pay back to his mother. And maybe find some validation in the process. Even finding a career that he was starting to love. He would handle this, too.

After a quick shower and breakfast, he met Cassie at the house so they could drive over in one car. She acquiesced to riding in his car so that the brothers could use the tools in her truck while they were gone. On the drive, she fidgeted in the seat. Maybe she was as nervous as he was. At a red light, he reached over and took her hand in his. "Whatever it is, we'll figure it out. We're in this together, right?"

She squeezed his hand and took a deep breath. "I don't think I slept much last night. You?"

"Not much."

"I keep wondering what they want to talk to us about."

"Another twist?"

She nodded. "That's what I figured, too. But what?"

He pulled into the parking structure next to the office building where the Belvedere

Foundation held offices. "I guess we're about to find out."

Mr. Belvedere greeted them as they stepped off the elevator. "Thank you for meeting with us on such short notice, Cassie, John."

"Of course."

"Such bad business with the damage to the houses over the weekend."

"Is that why we're here?"

Mr. Belvedere ushered them into a private office where a man and a woman sat in front of a large desk, two boys of about six playing with small cars on the carpet Mr. Belvedere introduced them to the young family. "Cassie and John, I'd like you to meet the Tanners."

Cassie nodded to them. "It's nice to meet you all."

"And you. I'm Donny, and this is my wife, Jo." She gave a soft smile. "And our twins, Milo and Gage."

John squatted beside the boys who looked up at him with open-eyed curiosity. "You boys like cars, huh?"

Jo made a noise and shook her head.

"Love them is more like it. We don't leave home without them."

Mr. Belvedere smiled warmly as he took a seat behind his desk. "This is the family that will own your house after the contest."

This announcement startled John more than he'd expected. "This is a twist."

"I did warn you they'd be coming." Mr. Belvedere smiled even wider. "You will now need to alter your design to meet the needs and wishes of the Tanner family. I'm sure they'll have ideas of what they're looking for." He checked his watch. "Another family is about to meet their design team, so I'll leave you all to get to know one another. John, once you've changed your specs, I'll expect copies to be delivered to me by the end of this week."

Nothing like the pressure of a deadline to make sweat break out on John's forehead, but he nodded. "Of course. Friday."

Mr. Belvedere left the office, and John took a seat beside Cassie. "As he said, I'm John, and this is Cassie. We've been working hard on the house. Your house."

Donny smiled and put his hand on Jo's shoulder. "We never thought that we'd own a house, so this is a surprise to us, as well. When the Belvedere Foundation called, we felt like we'd won the lottery."

"I should take notes about what you're looking for. If I had known we were meeting with you, I'd have brought my sketchbook." He pulled out his phone and opened the notes app. "So, what should I know about you all with respect to the house?"

Donny and Jo looked at each other and laughed. Jo said, "I'm not sure what to tell you."

Cassie suggested, "How about we start with your current home? Tell me what it's like."

They described a cramped one-bedroom apartment that had toys strewn in the living room because that had the most space for the twins to play. The boys slept in the bedroom while Donny and Jo shared the pull-out sofa at night. When John asked about the kitchen, Jo sighed. "When I dreamed of my own place, I thought it would have enough counter space to roll out the dough for Christmas cookies. And more than two burners to cook on."

Cassie nodded as John typed on his phone. "You're a cook, then?"

"I'd love to be able to create the meals my mother used to when I was growing up." She looked over at Donny. "We've been saving for a house since we got married, but it never seemed possible. There was always another bill waiting that ate up what we'd saved."

"So a big kitchen is on your list. Tell me what else you dreamed about for your first house."

John typed all their ideas into his phone. A tub big enough to bathe both boys at the same time. A master bedroom that would be their retreat at the end of the day. A backyard for the kids, and maybe a dog one day, to run around in. Enough room to invite their families over for the holidays. He wrote all of this down plus ideas of his own. He could see Jo cooking at the kitchen island they'd already planned. Donny working in the garage, showing the twins how to fix a car. And the decorated Christmas tree in the front window with the Tanner family posing for pictures much like the ones Loretta had shown him of the Czarnecks.

He discovered that Jo's favorite color was purple while Donny favored blue. The twins had a fascination with cars and trucks, making him glad that he'd saved the pedal car from the attic. And Donny worked two jobs so that Jo could work part-time at the library and still be at home and supervise their boys.

After almost an hour, John figured he had all he needed. He glanced at Cassie. "You have any other questions?"

She peered at the boys, then back at Jo. "What's most important to you to have in your dream home?"

Jo also looked at her children and sighed. "I've always wanted a home that would be a safe place for them to grow and learn. Size doesn't matter as much as that."

JO'S WORDS SEEMED to almost follow them as he and Cassie drove back to the house, discussing how they could make changes to their plans to meet the needs of the Tanners. This twist would make more work for him this week to get the new designs to Mr. Belvedere. While changes in deadlines before had brought him headaches, this had sparked a flame of creativity. John personally couldn't wait to start on the designs for the boys' bedrooms. After all, he understood a fascination with cars and trucks.

He pulled up in front of the house and turned in the seat to look at Cassie. "I hate to leave you all working here to go sketch, but these new design ideas are going to take up most of my time this week."

"It's fine, John." She gave him a shy smile. "But I will miss having you constantly underfoot when I'm trying to lay the new living room floor."

"Or tiling the bathroom?"

"Or picking out the new cabinets."

"You wouldn't dare do it without me."

They smiled at each other for a long moment until Tiny tapped on the passenger window. "Hey, boss lady. Are you planning to work today? Or do Biggie and I have to pick up your slack?"

Cassie made a wry smile. "Give me just a second."

Tiny shook his head and walked up to the front door. Cassie turned back to John. "So, listen, don't be a stranger. I admit I've gotten used to your face."

Then she opened the door and exited the car before he could say another word.

CASSIE SAT UP straight in the plastic molded chair next to the detective's desk as he read through a file, glancing up at her several times as he did so. She spotted his nameplate. Tyler Matthews. Once he was finished with the file, he closed it and pulled a notepad and pen from a drawer. "Ms. Lowman, I appreciate you coming down to talk to me about this unfortunate business. Thankfully, the damage done to the contest houses isn't too severe."

"No problem. I'm happy to help. I have nothing to hide." He had interviewed the Buttucci brothers that morning, so she had expected him to call her in for questioning shortly thereafter.

The detective nodded but didn't look at her. Instead he wrote her name along with the date. "You understand that you're not being accused of anything at this time."

At this time. She felt her insides drop into her shoes at his words. As if she could be accused at a later date. This was so frustrating. She hadn't done anything. "I understand."

"The Buttucci brothers were adamant this morning that you weren't involved in the vandalism."

"They're right. I'm not."

He nodded and wrote some words on the notepad as she took in the busy precinct. "Aren't you going to take me into an interrogation room like they do on TV?"

He grinned but shook his head. "Like I said, you're not being accused. I'm simply trying to get more information about what happened." He looked at a clock on the wall. "We're just waiting for someone to join us. And of course, he's late."

"Who?" Her first thought was John, but if he'd been asked to come down to the station, he would have said so earlier when she'd called to check in on his progress with the sketches. Maybe Nick? He seemed to be convinced that she was guilty.

A man in a rumpled suit walked over to the detective's desk and took a seat next to Cassie. "Ms. Lowman."

It was George August, the detective from

her father's case. She looked back at Tyler. "Why is he here?"

George held his hands up as if he were surrendering. "Tyler called me when he saw your name. Thought I might be able to give him some insight into his case."

"You have nothing to do with this case." She scooted her chair a few inches away from the one George sat in. "My father has nothing to do with what happened."

"Maybe. Maybe not. But you have to admit that the name Lowman keeps popping up. And not in a good way."

If she thought things were frustrating before, George's appearance made it even more so. Did they think, like the other contestants did, that because her father was accused of crimes his daughter would be as culpable? She closed her eyes and took a few deep breaths. "I would never purposely ruin what my team has been doing. Damage the house I'm working my butt off to renovate. Winning this contest means I can start my own company. I wouldn't do anything to jeopardize that."

George leaned back in the chair and put his hands behind his head. "To be honest,

Ms. Lowman, I don't think you did it. Neither does Tyler. But we have some other questions."

Tyler cleared his throat. "Do you know where your father is, Cassie?"

She stared at the two men. "Is that why you brought me down here? To ask me about my father again?"

"We have reason to believe he's in the area. Would he try to sabotage the houses in order to give you an advantage over the competition?"

Cassie glared at George. "No. If that was the case, why would he trash my house, too?"

"When's the last time you heard from him?"

She considered lying about the phone call she had received but realized that it was pointless. George acted as if he seemed to already know about it. Had her mother told him? She swallowed and clasped her hands together. "Last week. To congratulate me on making it into the contest. I'm sorry, I should have told you. But with the demo starting and the project going full tilt—"

"Come on, Ms. Lowman." George looked skeptical. "You couldn't find a minute to report this?"

"There was no point." She pulled her phone out and swiped it open, locating the date and time of the call. She handed the phone to the detective. "The call lasted only a few seconds."

George peered at her phone, then recorded the details for himself. "You still should have told us about it right after it happened. Are you trying to hide his whereabouts?"

"No!"

He gave her phone back to her, stood and walked away, pressing his own phone to his ear. Tyler sighed and doodled on the notepad. "He said he wasn't going to take over the interview. But I pretty much expected this from George. He's like a dog with a bone and won't give up."

"Do you really think my dad was the one who caused the trouble at the houses?"

Tyler shook his head. "No. Evidence suggests it was someone connected to the contest. Someone who knew when the crews would be finished for the day." He looked at her. "How much do you know about the Buttucci brothers?"

"They're like family. They wouldn't do this, either."

"Did you know about their ties to the Holisters? They're bad news in this state."

Cassie cleared her throat. "Their mother was a Holister, but Tiny and Biggie are not involved in the way you're thinking."

"Hmm. And yet, here they are with a number of Holisters." He pulled out pictures of the brothers surrounded by what must have been family members, and pushed them along the desk's surface toward her. She picked up the top one. "You're wrong. They have relatives that have been convicted before, but they're clean. They worked hard for my father and now for me."

Detective August rejoined them. "And doesn't that make you pause and wonder how your father was able to hide the money he was embezzling from the company? How he learned to be able to hide his crimes for years?"

Her father wouldn't do that. He'd been proud of how far he'd come by the sweat of his own brow and wouldn't jeopardize the company he'd started before she'd been born.

Would he?

If she was wrong about her father, could she be just as deluded about the Buttucci brothers? Tiny and Biggie watched over her like favorite uncles. They knew how important winning this contest was to her, and by extension them. She picked up another photo and studied it. It seemed to show money exchanging hands between Tiny and one of the Holisters.

She shot to her feet and shook her head. "Are we done here? I don't think there's anything more to say."

Tyler handed her a business card with his phone numbers. "If you think of anything else to share, call me."

She pocketed the card. "I get what you believe about my father, Detective August, but he's just not capable of the things you're accusing him of."

"The truth is that you don't want to think he's guilty, but I have ironclad proof that he is." He held out his arm and ushered her to the front door of the precinct. "If you hear from your father again, I need you to tell me right away. Not days after the fact."

She raised an eyebrow. "Ironclad?"

He gave her a curt nod and opened the door for her to pass through. She left, wondering how she could be so wrong about the people she loved.

JOHN SURVEYED THE empty house. Being here when the brothers and Cassie were gone made him feel as if he was intruding into someone else's life. He had initially thought about staying home to rework the designs but wanted to visualize his ideas in the space before finalizing them. He stood in the room that would be for one of the twins and closed his eyes. They liked cars and trucks, so what if he made each of the boy's bedrooms like a mechanic's garage? Trucks. Tools. Bold colors in red, yellow and black, and green, blue and white.

"Hello in the house," a voice called out.

John opened his eyes and walked into the living room. A man with a clipboard stood in the entryway. "I'm Darren, from the city. Electrical inspection. I'm scheduled to do this place tomorrow, but as

I'm in the neighborhood now, thought I'd squeeze it in. Okay?"

"Sure." Cassie had mentioned that an inspector would be out to hopefully give preliminary approval before they completed the wiring. "Anything you need me to do? I'm John Robison, the designer for the house. Cassie, the contractor, had a meeting this morning. Otherwise, she'd be here."

Darren shook his head and held up a small rectangular gadget. "Got all I need. I'll be about twenty to thirty minutes."

John nodded and returned to the first of the twins' rooms, but the image he'd pictured so clearly before the interruption had faded. He took a seat on the plywood subfloor and picked up his sketchpad and pencil to try to recreate what he'd seen.

Time passed quickly as he drew and erased lines. A knock on the doorframe brought his attention back to the present and the electrical inspector standing over him. The man tore a sheet off the clipboard and handed it to John. "I made notations on things that have to be replaced or upgraded before I can sign off on the electrical work."

John glanced at the page and nodded, not understanding what it all meant and wishing that Cassie was there to make sense of this. "Cassie already made the upgrades."

"My notes indicate where she needs to go back before the final inspection."

He started to leave, but John followed him, holding aloft the page. "Are you saying she did it wrong?"

The inspector turned and sighed. "Listen. This is normal. I inspect. Make notes. She fixes it. I inspect again. End of story."

"But she's licensed. Why wouldn't she get it right the first time?" He had had faith in her that she knew what was she doing. What if she didn't? What if all the self-doubts she'd been having were real, and he'd been as duped to believe in her?

Darren waved him off. "Overall, you've passed. You're fine, okay?"

John tried to decipher the notes on the page, realizing he had a lot left to learn about renovating a house as opposed to designing a hybrid sedan. "Okay."

Darren nodded and left the house, passing Cassie as she entered. She glanced behind her at the retreating back of the inspector. "Did we pass?"

John handed her the inspection notice. "Overall, yes."

She read the page and snapped her fingers. "Shoot. I figured that one circuit in the bathroom might need to be changed out, but not the entire half of the house. This adds another day to our schedule."

"I don't understand."

Cassie looked confused. "Understand what?"

"If you knew the circuit might need to be changed, why didn't you? Why are we wasting time redoing the electrical that you assured me you knew how to do?" He paced the length of the living room and came to a stop right in front of her. "I might be new to home design, but you're not. Why the mistakes?"

"Mistakes?" She held up the page, waving it in his face. "These are not mistakes. These are recommendations. The circuits in this house are more damaged than I had expected, but that doesn't mean I rewired them wrong."

"Darren said this was normal."

"It is." She crossed her arms over her chest and looked him in the eye. "Are you starting to worry about my abilities?"

"You've been doubting mine from the first."

They stared at each other for a long moment. Finally, Cassie sighed and dropped her arms to her sides. "I've got enough to do without adding this to my problems."

Noticing her furrowed brow, he said, "The police?"

She dug through a knapsack she had and produced a handful of papers. "It's nothing. I just need to get my hands dirty and my thoughts on this project instead. I'm sure you have plenty to do, as well."

She left the living room and he took it as his cue to get back to work. He returned to the twins' bedrooms. The atmosphere in the house hung heavy with tension. Even the volume on the radio in the hallway had been turned down as John sketched and Cassie rewired the bathroom and master bedroom. The sound of a car horn honking brought both of them outside.

Tiny motioned to the back of the brothers' truck. "I think I found our replacement kitchen cabinets. Come see."

John approached the truck with a mix of hope and dread. They'd been searching for days but hadn't found what they were looking for. Would this be another case of disappointment? But the closer he got to the truck, the more excited he became. The golden color of the oak in the cabinets matched the picture of the kitchen in his head and his sketch. The lines of the cabinets were simple and clean. He put a hand on one of the upper cupboards and nodded. Solid.

Cassie joined him at the truck bed and bit her lip as she moved her hands along the surfaces. "The glass fronts are missing."

"Easy enough to replace," Tiny told her. "Biggie has worked with cupboards in worse condition."

"They're going to need a lot of sanding and restaining before we can install them. More work than if we buy prefabricated."

John murmured, "These are exactly what we've been looking for. Where did you find them, Tiny?"

"A friend of mine mentioned that his

cousin was rehabbing a house out in the suburbs and was getting rid of them." He shrugged. "I got these for a song."

Cassie peered at Tiny. "Which friend?"

Tiny eyed his brother before facing her. "You don't know him."

"I need a name," she insisted.

Tiny's eyebrows rose as he looked over at Cassie. "What did the detective tell you?"

John glanced between them. "Detective?"

Tiny answered instead. "The police seem to think that our extended family makes us real suspects for sabotaging the contest houses. And maybe helping your father get away with embezzlement."

Tiny glared at Cassie. "Do you think we're guilty?"

"I don't know what to think."

This admission from her shocked John as well as the brothers, who gaped. "You know us, Cassie. We are honest, hardworking guys who have loved you and your dad for years. Why would we hurt your chances of winning the contest?" Tiny asked.

"Maybe you're trying to help me by hurting the others. You have to admit that the damage to our house was mostly cosmetic."

Tiny gritted his teeth and pounded the truck before walking away from them. Biggie blinked several times before turning to go after his brother. John whistled. "What just happened? You don't think they'd really do this."

Cassie sniffed and shook her head. "I don't want to believe it. But what if my faith in them is as misguided as that in my dad? How could I be so wrong about the people in my life?"

John put a hand on her shoulder, but she stiffened and took a step away. "Cass, they're right about these cabinets. They'll be a perfect fit with the layout and design."

"What if they got them through illegal means?"

"Buying them from a contractor who was probably going to toss them otherwise? Sounds legit to me."

"We have to be aboveboard on everything for this contest. I can't let the scandal surrounding my father and his business taint what we're trying to do here." She shook her head. "If they'd only give me a name and I could verify their story."

"Jim Sanders," Biggie offered as he returned to them.

Cassie nodded. "I hate that these detectives made me distrust you. I'm sorry. I don't know what to believe anymore."

"You can believe in us." Biggie wrapped his beefy arms around her small frame. "We'll figure it out."

He placed a kiss on the top of her head, and John smiled. The big man might be quiet and gruff, but he could see how much he loved Cassie. Tiny rejoined their group. "I'll prove our innocence to you, Cass. You won't ever have to doubt us again."

CHAPTER SEVEN

THE HOUSE WAS coming along, but the way Cassie figured it they were still behind. The Fourth of July was looming, and she needed to ask the team to give up their holiday to work in order to meet the deadline.

A familiar truck pulled up in front of the house, and she groaned and wished that she could start the day over. Bad enough that it had started to rain and she'd had to leave Evie in the mudroom by herself. And they'd run out of coffee beans yesterday, and she'd forgotten to pick up more before coming to the house that morning. The caffeine withdrawal headache throbbed as she went to the front door and opened it to greet Mr. Clemens.

"Are you sure you want to inspect the plumbing under the house today in this rain?" she asked, although she already knew his answer.

"I'm tight for time, Ms. Lowman. I don't have any to waste on doing what I want to do, but only on what I have to do." He glanced at the bare living room that still didn't have drywall. "I'll check around here before going down in the crawl space."

"Give me a warning before you get to the mudroom."

He eyed her and frowned. She was tempted to give him a salute, but she tamped down her sarcastic tendencies and focused on checking the electrical socket that she had to rewire. Mr. Clemens passed by her to examine the pipes in the bathroom and muttered under his breath before marking things off on his clipboard.

She heard him in the kitchen next. He wouldn't open the door to the mudroom before letting her know, would he? The bark and the yelp that followed told her he had. She sprinted into the kitchen to find him backed into a corner while Evie tried to sniff him and make friends. "I told you to warn me before going in there."

He pointed a shaking finger at the dog. "Get that thing away from me."

Cassie smiled and gave Evie a good

rub. "She's only trying to say hello." Evie panted, and it seemed to Cassie that she almost smiled at the fussy plumbing inspector who still looked anxious before her. "How about I hold her while you check the mudroom?"

He gave a short nod as Cassie held on to Evie's collar. When the dog tried to follow the inspector, Cassie crouched by her and rubbed behind her ears. "You wouldn't hurt the inspector, would you?"

The dog made a noise as if to say she'd never think of doing that. Mr. Clemens stepped softly out of the mudroom and took the long route to the front door.

"Come on. Back to the mudroom for now. Once my tools are out of your way, you can have full rein of the house. Okay, girl?"

Evie barked her agreement and Cassie shut the door. "Only another fifteen minutes, and then you can come back out."

A few moments later, a knock on the front door announced the return of Mr. Clemens. Cassie invited him in, but he opted to stay on the porch. "Plumbing's fine. Someone will be out to inspect again once the fixtures are in place."

"You won't be coming back?"

The man seemed to pale even more. "I'll have an associate of mine take over this particular project." Then he practically ran next door.

SATURDAY WAS ANOTHER WORKDAY. Not that John minded. He didn't have much else happening outside of his work on the house at the moment. He'd thrown his entire self into the project like he always did whenever he was involved in a new car design. Maybe some things didn't change even if the object of his efforts had.

Since they'd passed the electrical inspection, they could now start to hang drywall. Although he'd never done anything like this, he rather enjoyed holding up the walls while one of the brothers secured them into place. Then it was his job to mud the seams. With the walls going up, the house was starting to take shape. Tiny said that once the mud over the seams was dry, they would sand the walls and prep them for paint.

Someone called his name from the living room. Seeing the Tanner family standing at the entryway, John held up his hand in welcome. "Donny, Jo, come to see the house?"

Jo said, "I couldn't wait. My parents have the boys for the day, so we figured, why not? I know you said it was a mess, but I just had to see it."

Cassie entered from the kitchen, stopped short and smiled. "Anxious to see what we've done for you? Want the nickel tour?"

John stood back and Cassie took over. She pointed out the details that had been completed and how they fit with those that were still to come. Jo especially loved the picture window in the living room. In the kitchen, they had to imagine a lot of what would be there since it was still a work in progress. Cassie showed them paint chips as well as samples for the tile backsplash and pulled out one of the square tiles that would eventually cover the floor.

John led the tour when it came to the bedrooms. Jo nodded as he talked about the garage concept for the boys' rooms. "They're going to love it."

The one thing he didn't share was his

idea for building a wooden ramp along one wall with a connecting tunnel between the rooms that the boys could use to zoom their cars around. He figured that would be one surprise for the final reveal. He guided them into the guest room and sensed Donny's hesitation. "You don't want a guest room?"

The man shrugged. "I guess it's fine."

"If you want to change things, now is the time to say so."

Donny winced. "I guess I don't see the need for a guest room. We don't have many that sleep over since everyone's local."

Cassie asked, "What would you like to use this room for?"

Jo gave Donny an encouraging bob of her head. "We don't need an office since my work is with cars at the garage and Jo's at the library part-time. And like I said, I doubt we would use a guest room. But we'd love to have a TV room." He spread his hands along where a wall would be. "Big-screen TV here. A comfy couch that the family could sink into while we watch our favorite shows and movies."

"Instead of in the living room?" John wanted to verify.

Donny nodded. "It'd be nice to have the living room be for conversation rather than having our eyes glued to a television."

Cassie looked at John, who had to agree. "No problem. We'll make the change." He already had ideas percolating about how to repurpose the space and use the technology package the foundation had provided.

Tour completed, they strolled into the backyard and checked out the garage that housed most of the construction supplies. "Don't worry. This will all be out of here before you move in." Cassie shifted a couple of cans of paint out of their path. "It will hold one car, plus have plenty of space for storage. Bikes, a lawn mower, garbage cans."

Jo loved the huge maple tree in the backyard. "I can imagine the boys climbing this when they get a bit older." She pointed to a patch of ground where John had turned over the soil and transplanted a few tomato plants. "A garden?"

"One of the neighbors talked about how she used to grow some of their food. I wondered if that's something you would be interested in."

"I never thought of it before, and I have no experience."

"Would you be willing to learn?"

She shrugged and laughed. "Why not? This is a gift I didn't expect. The boys might like to help me weed and water it."

"You'll be moving in after the growing season, but I thought I could prepare it for next spring's planting. I could come back to help you. It's something I'm just learning about myself."

Jo held out her hand to John and they shook on it. "Deal."

They returned to the living room. Donny put his arm around his wife's shoulders, and they looked out the large window at their new neighborhood. They didn't say anything for a long while, but when Jo turned back to look at Cassie and John, she had tears in her eyes. "I can't thank you enough for the work you're putting into this house. Even in this state, I can see the potential and know that you'll make it amazing."

Cassie put her hand on Jo's shoulder and rubbed it. "It's our honor. And you're welcome to stop by anytime."

"I think we'd like to keep the rest a surprise," Donny said, smiling. "Thank you for the tour. We'll let you get back to your work."

After the Tanners left, John felt as if he'd been reenergized. Even though he'd had a long week of work, he felt as if he could put in another twelve-hour day and still feel good. The Tanners' visit reminded him of why he had agreed to do the contest in the first place. Part of it was to prove that he could use his designs in a new arena, but now the bigger part had come to mean giving back to the community. And more specifically, to provide the dream home to the Tanners, who deserved the blessing.

THE BUTTUCCIS HAD a potential job to bid on after this one was completed, so they left early. It was just herself and John at the house. Without the brothers' help, Cassie had to depend on John when she needed strong arms to hold up a slab of drywall as she fastened it to the wood frame. She called his name, but he didn't respond. She went looking for him and found him in the newly designated TV room. He had his sketchpad on his knees as he sat on the floor, drawing. He looked up as she stood in the doorway. "Sorry. Did you need me?"

"It can wait." She peered over his shoulder at the sketch. "Talk about throwing us a twist, huh?"

He mumbled something since his focus was on the picture and not on her. She watched as he transformed what they had planned to be a plain wall to hang artwork into a row of unique built-in bookcases. He added the requested comfy couch and two smaller beanbags that she assumed were for the boys. "Nice."

He held the sketch up for her to see. "I think I got it." He rose to his feet. "You said something about help?"

He followed her into the kitchen where she pointed at the drywall. "I need you to hold that in place while I nail it to the wall."

He hefted the slab and positioned it to where she indicated. She stood on the ladder and used her nail gun to secure it into place. "One down. Three more to go."

He let go of the drywall as she came down the ladder and pointed to another, ready to be installed. He stood so close to her that she could smell the soap he'd used. She tried to ignore the odd way it made her heart trip. They repeated the process until they were done and stood back to admire their work. "It's coming along."

"But not as quickly as you'd hoped," he said.

"I'm thinking of hiring some extra help to get the last of the drywall finished. We'll never make the deadline at this rate."

"I'm committed to do whatever we have to."

"I know. I appreciate that."

He reached over and pushed a strand of hair behind her ear. She swallowed and kept her gaze on his before he looked away, scanning the kitchen. "So, what's next?"

Her stomach growled and she put a hand to it with a grimace. Checking her watch, she groaned. "Is it really after five already?"

"Why? Do you have a date?"

"Hard to remember what those are since it's been so long." She noticed the corners of his mouth twitch, that he appeared happy at her words. "How about you?" she asked.

"My fiancée broke up with me when I

got laid off. Seems that being out of work wasn't part of her plan for our life."

"Ouch."

He sounded casual about it, as if it didn't matter, but she could see what it had cost him. Probably had hit his ego as much as losing his job had.

"Do you mind if we bring dinner in and keep working? I'd like to get a little more finished here before calling it a night."

"I'll do you one better. Let's work another two hours, then I'll treat you to dinner out at a place with actual tables and chairs."

That sounded amazing. A real dinner that didn't come out of a box or wrapper? She looked down at her T-shirt, which was marked with some of the mud she'd used earlier that day. At her jeans, which had a large hole on one knee and a rip along her calf. "I'm not exactly dressed for going out to dinner."

"We can go home, shower and change and then meet at the restaurant. How does the Lotus sound?"

Man, he was really trying hard to get her to go out with him. The Lotus served her favorite Chinese food, though she tended to get carryout instead. Besides, going to a restaurant with John felt like a date. Tempting… "As good as that sounds, I'd rather eat here and then keep working. Okay? I don't want to lose our momentum."

"I'll bring Lotus here then. What's your poison?"

She gave him her order, and he called it in. A half hour later, they sat on the steps in the backyard to eat their dinners, Evie at their feet waiting for any morsels that might fall. She pulled out a pair of wooden chopsticks as well as her carton of sesame chicken and dug into it. They must have both been hungry since they ate without words for a while, the chirp of crickets the only soundtrack for their summer evening.

Finally, she broke the silence. "Thank you for dinner. This really hits the spot." He nodded as he continued eating his lo mein. She put her carton beside her on the step and leaned back. "This is really a nice place. Almost better than any restaurant with linen tablecloths and crystal goblets."

"You enjoy the simple things."

She gave a one-shoulder shrug. "Some things."

"Most things. I don't know any other woman who is more content to be covered in sawdust."

"It's what I grew up with."

"So did your sister, but only you followed in your father's footsteps."

What he said was true, but she didn't want to dwell on it just then. She stuck the chopsticks into her carton, her appetite gone. "I wanted to be just like him, but the man I thought I knew might be a crook. It's hard. And has hurt my family badly." She looked over at him. "Can we change the subject?"

"Why does this contest really mean so much to you? Is it just to redeem your family name?"

It had been at first. She had wanted nothing more than to prove that a Lowman could be honest and full of integrity. Could create a beautiful living space. That she was a good person as well as a fantastic builder. "I feel like my life was put on hold when my father's supposed crimes came to light. His company had to cease and desist while the investigators sifted through its records. This meant I had no job. And that job was my whole life, so I had nothing. The contest was announced at the right time. I thought if I could win it, then I could find a life outside of my father. Work that meant something, which in turn would mean I was worth something, too." She stared out into the backyard. "Pathetic, isn't it?"

"Sounds about right. Switch your dad with my employer, and we're in the same exact place." He sighed and stretched out. "I needed purpose, and the contest seems to provide that."

"What if we don't win?"

"We can't think that way. We have to focus on being the best and proving to them all that we're just as good as they are."

She rested her hand on his. "You are good. Better than good. You blow me away with your ideas and how positive you are. It's been my privilege to work with you."

He reached out and touched her cheek. "The privilege has been all mine."

She dropped her gaze from his, aware of how vulnerable she'd made herself to him.

Wondering if he would accept her words, accept her. And why did it matter so much that he would?

"Cass," he breathed her name before he pressed his lips against hers.

She closed her eyes and reveled in the feel of his kiss. Pressed into him, deepening the embrace and thrusting her hands into his curly hair. It was soft when she'd expected coarse. Her hands moved to his broad shoulders, and she tugged him closer until he held her just as tightly.

She could have sat on the back step and kissed him forever, but they had work to do if they wanted to win.

And they both had good, complicated reasons to do just that.

CHAPTER EIGHT

JOHN WOKE UP Sunday morning with thoughts of Cassie's mouth on his. He hadn't meant to kiss her, but her sweet innocence and raw honesty had drawn him to her until he couldn't resist the temptation any longer. She had finally ended their kisses with a reminder that they ought to be hammering and painting. And reluctantly, he'd agreed.

But not before stealing one more kiss.

He rolled onto his back and put his arm over his eyes. What had he been thinking? Mixing business with pleasure had never lead to anywhere good. Or lasting.

The sun had started to rise, creating streaks of light across his ceiling. He should get up and get ready, but maybe he'd stay in bed for just another moment and relive those kisses.

Because they wouldn't be happening again.

The day stretched out before him with nothing planned. Despite the work that still needed to be done and their looming deadline, the four of them had elected to give themselves the day off. To reset. Reenergize.

He'd been going so hard on the house lately that his free time had disappeared to the point that he didn't know what to do now that he had some. Most of his friends had families that preoccupied them. Maybe he could call his cousin and see if he wanted to hang out.

Instead, John ended up at the house with the idea of planning the design of the garage. Without the whine of saws and tapping of hammers, the neighborhood was quiet. The residential area had mostly single family homes with mature trees lining the street. Miss Loretta had told him that an elementary school sat in the middle of the neighborhood three streets over, so many young families had once lived here. When the housing bubble hit, many folks lost their homes and most had sat empty ever since. It was only in the last few years that working families had started to move back.

He opened the garage door and stared inside. At the moment, it was still full of supplies for fixing up the house. He moved things around to make a path toward the back wall.

Pushing a box of tiles aside, he heard a noise coming from the house. He hadn't seen any cars or trucks nearly, so no one should be inside. Remembering the trouble that had happened earlier, he pulled a two-by-four from the bin of scraps. He brandished the hunk of wood like a baseball bat and walked into the backyard. Opening the metal gate of the fence, he then crept up the stairs and quietly opened the back door. He stepped inside the mudroom. His heart beat out of his chest and a thrumming rang in his ears as he moved into the kitchen and saw the ax buried into the cabinet that waited to be installed.

He put his hand on the deep gash and barely registered the dark blur before something hard struck the back of his head.

CASSIE PULLED UP behind a police car and an ambulance, its lights flashing. She hopped out of her truck and ran to where John sat on the porch steps with a towel pressed to his nape. The police officer put up a hand out to stop her from rushing up to hug him. "I'm with John. He called me."

John looked up at her, and she noticed the pain reflected in his eyes. She squatted before him. "What happened?"

"I dropped by to get a better sense of the garage space. Spark some ideas. An intruder got the jump on me."

"How are you? Are you all right?" Cassie put her hand on his knee. "Did the paramedics look at you?" She moved to check the abrasion on the back of his head.

She started to remove the towel when John grabbed her wrist. "Cass, it gets worse."

"What could be worse than you getting hurt?" She glanced at the police officer. "More sabotage?" She closed her eyes, then ran into the house. The living room looked okay. No spray paint or garbage. She ran down the hallway, peeking into each room. Nothing there. She returned to the living room and moved through the arch to the kitchen and gasped.

Every one of the cabinets they'd planned to install had been smashed, an ax buried deep into the surfaces and one of the doors. She started to reach out for the handle and remove the ax but remembered the cops would want to check for fingerprints.

Why would anyone do this? Just to make it harder for them to win? Or was it someone who didn't want the contest to be in their neighborhood? The possibilities made her head hurt. The police officer behind her cleared his throat. "Sorry, Ms. Lowman, but I need you to come outside. The technician is here to process the crime scene."

Her house was a crime scene. She gave a nod and reluctantly left the kitchen.

She joined John on the porch and sat next to him on the top step. "I don't understand why this is happening to us." She turned to look at him. "How's the head?"

"The paramedic wants me to get checked out at the hospital, but I told her I'd be fine."

Cassie stood and waved over the paramedic. "Does he need to go to the hospital?"

"That's what I told him, but he refused treatment."

Cassie tugged on his arm and pulled him to his feet. "That's it, mister. I'll drive you myself if you won't go in the ambulance, but you are going to the hospital."

"I'm okay."

Cassie removed the towel and winced at the blood that trickled down his neck. "No, that needs to get looked at." To the paramedic, she said, "I'll make sure he gets there. Thank you."

John sighed. "I really don't want to go."

"And I really don't want to replace all those cabinets, but we both have to do what we have to do." Back inside the house, the policeman stood over the photographer, pointing out angles to take pictures. He turned to her when she tapped his shoulder. "I need to take John to the hospital. I'm sure you'll have questions for us later."

"Yes, ma'am. I'll follow up with you both then."

She walked out and linked her arm with John's to bring him to her truck. She opened the passenger door and was about to help him up, but he stepped back. "I can get in by myself."

"Then do it."

He grumbled but got in and allowed her to buckle his seat belt. "It's no big deal."

"You could have a concussion, and I'm not taking any chances." She slammed his door shut and ran around the truck to get in the driver's side. She started the truck and carefully backed out of the driveway to avoid hitting the folks who'd congregated on the sidewalk. "I can't believe we got hit by this jerk again. And that you startled him in the process." She turned on to the avenue and started driving toward the hospital. "Did you see who it was?"

"No, he was behind me. I didn't see a thing. And when I came to, he was gone."

"Is there anyone you want me to call? Your mom, maybe?"

"Definitely not my mom. I don't want to worry her."

The drive to the hospital didn't take long, and Cassie pulled her truck in front of the entrance to the emergency room. "You go in, and I'll park."

"You don't have to stay with me."

"Nice try. I'm not leaving until you see the doctor."

He shot her a dark look but got out of the truck and entered the ER. She found a spot at the edge of the lot and soon joined

John in the waiting area. There were quite a few people ahead of them, and Cassie wondered if she should call her mom to let her know she'd be missing Sunday dinner. She glanced at her watch, noting it was a little after two. Hours yet.

JOHN SAT, STRETCHING his leg muscles just as Cassie checked her watch again. "Need to be somewhere?"

"How long does it take to get looked at? It's been over an hour." She leaned back in the plastic chair and slumped down. "I hate these places."

"I told you that you didn't have to wait with me." But part of him was glad she had stayed. He didn't like hospitals any more than she did.

She eyed him and shook her head before crossing her arms over her chest. "You're stuck with me."

"John Robison," a female voice called out.

He signaled to the nurse and got to his feet, but it must have been too fast, because he swayed. Luckily, Cassie was there to put her arms around his middle and hold him upright. "Whoa there. Still think you don't need to see a doctor?"

"I stood up too quickly."

"Uh-huh."

The nurse who had called his name brought over a wheelchair, but he shook his head. He might be woozy but he wasn't an invalid that needed to get pushed around. "I can walk just fine."

The nurse and Cassie both pointed to the wheelchair, and he growled as the nurse wheeled him into an exam room. "Miss, can you help me get him onto the exam table?"

Having Cassie so close as she put her arms around his waist and guided him onto the bed felt like sweet torture. He buried his face in her hair and inhaled the pretty scent.

Cassie pulled back, her hand on the top of her head. "Did you just sniff me?"

He managed a small grin.

She took a seat in a metal chair next to the bed as the nurse recorded his vitals on her tablet. "Mr. Robison, the intake nurse said you hit your head."

"Someone blindsided him on the back of the head. With what we don't know."

The nurse wrote down the notes. "Did you lose consciousness?"

Cassie replied for him again. "Yes, he did, but he doesn't know for how long. He called me right after he woke up." She shifted to look at him directly. "I told you before, there are reasons we don't go alone to the job site."

John tried to seem casual, though he had to admit he appreciated Cassie's fierce concern for him. "I didn't expect to be in any danger."

She rolled her eyes and the nurse continued her questions. "Headache? Nausea? Vomiting?"

"He complained about a headache on the way over here."

The nurse looked at John. It didn't seem that he needed to answer any questions with Cassie around. "What she said. But no vomiting."

"Nausea, then?" He managed to nod, and she made more notes on her tablet. "The doctor will be in to see you shortly, Mr. Robison. You're lucky to have your wife with you. She told me a lot more quickly than you did."

"She's not my wife," he said but the nurse had already left and pulled the curtain shut behind her.

Cassie's cheeks were pink when he looked back at her. "I can't believe you took such a risk, John. You knew there was a vandal running around the neighborhood, and you went in alone to check out a noise?"

Concerned Cassie had been replaced by an angry version. "I couldn't let them do any more damage."

"So you call 911. You don't run into danger, especially by yourself."

He closed his eyes, but the room started to spin. Not good. Opening his eyes, he rested his head against the pillows. "Do you have to be so loud?"

"I get loud when I'm irritated."

"Can you go back to being sweet and worried?"

The curtain was swept aside, and a young doctor with short curly hair, wearing pastel pink scrubs, entered the room. "Mr. Robison, I'm Dr. April Harrison. Nancy told me that you're showing symptoms of a concussion after getting hit on the head. Can I see the wound?"

He gritted his teeth as the doctor's fingers gently probed against his neck. "That's quite a wound you've got. Looks like you'll need a few stitches. Then I'm sending you for a head CT."

"Is that necessary?"

"It's likely a concussion, but I want to rule out a closed head injury, which could make things get serious really quickly." She shone a light in his eyes, and he winced at its brightness. "Now follow my finger with your eyes." He did so. "And now squeeze my fingers with yours. Good."

Once the examination was over, the doctor explained, "We had a multiple car accident earlier, so the wait for your CT scan could be a while. In the meantime, I'll have Nancy suture your wound and give you something for the pain."

"Thank you, Doctor."

She turned to Cassie. "We'll have your husband as good as new in no time."

"She's not my wife," he exclaimed, then winced. "Just a friend," he clarified in a barely-there whisper.

Dr. Harrison looked at them with some amusement. "I stand corrected." Then she left them alone.

Cassie moved to his side. "Why do they keep thinking we're married?"

"Probably because we sound like it."

She sighed and put her hand on his arm. "I didn't mean to yell at you, but I was scared. What if this creep had done more than just knock you out? This partnership doesn't work without you."

He swallowed and stared into her eyes until he got dizzy and had to close his own. "I'm going to be here a while if you want to take off now. They won't let me go until they're done with their tests."

"No, I'm staying. I just need to make a quick call."

As she left the room with her cell phone, the nurse returned with a tray of scary-looking needles. He grimaced at the sight of them. He'd never been very good with needles, and the nausea he'd been feeling intensified. "I think I'm going to be sick."

IT WAS AFTER seven that evening by the time John was released into Cassie's care. Because of his concussion, he couldn't stay alone but needed to be woken every couple of hours. He protested when she volunteered to go home with him, but Dr. Harrison overruled him. "You need someone with you just in case. And your friend here doesn't look like she'll take no for an answer."

Cassie pulled the truck up to the ER entrance and assisted him into her vehicle. He gave her directions to his apartment, but she waved them off. "I've been there before, remember? I know the way."

"What are you going to do about your dog?"

"I called my sister. She took Evie home with her."

She had to drive down his street twice before she admitted defeat and double-parked in front of his building. "I'll have to let you off here and then drive further to park."

"I can walk."

"I'm not taking a chance." They exited her vehicle and she made sure he'd wait in the lobby and not be so stubborn as to go up to his apartment on his own. She ran back out to her truck to find a parking spot for the night.

Surprised to find John still sitting in the lobby, she whistled. "You're getting better at listening to directions."

"Maybe I'm too tired to fight with you."

He stood, and she put her arms around his waist. She was so much shorter than him, but he put his arm around her shoulder, and they ambled to the elevators.

Once she got him to his apartment door, he fumbled with the keys until she took them from him and unlocked the door. "To the couch or to bed?"

"My bed, thanks. I can barely keep my eyes open."

As they shuffled down the hallway, she thought of making a joke about him finally inviting her inside his bedroom but figured he wasn't in the mood. They got to the foot of the bed, and he collapsed on top. Carefully, she helped him get comfortable. She removed his shoes, then looked at his jeans. Should she volunteer to take them off for him?

"Leave them on," he said, answering the unspoken question.

"You might be more relaxed with them off."

"I'm not letting you take off my clothes." He closed his eyes and put an arm to his forehead. "I'm letting you off the hook. You can go home now."

"Nice try." She noticed the tall dresser near the closet with beveled doors. "I'll get you some shorts to change yourself into after I leave the room. Is that okay?"

"Fine. Third dresser drawer."

She noted that he'd painted the walls an indigo blue, similar to hers. While it made the room dark and appear smaller than it was, it also made it feel like she was co-cooned and safe, which was the effect she'd wanted in her bedroom. Finding a pair of shorts with an elastic waist, she pulled them out and laid them on the bed beside John. The bed was large and had several pillows lined up against the wrought iron headboard. Maybe she could do something like that in her bedroom.

John moaned, and her focus immediately switched back to him. "Do you need some pain medication?" The doctor had sent them home with a prescription that she had

had filled at the hospital's pharmacy. The medicine now waited in the small white paper bag John had flung on to the nightstand before lying on the bed.

"Please."

She left the bedroom and found a cut crystal glass in the bathroom and filled it with water from the faucet. Returning, she noted that John had propped himself on several pillows. She handed him the glass of water and a couple of tablets, which he swallowed. His eyes closed, and she helped him lie back down. Looking around the room, she didn't see a blanket, so she pulled the comforter over him from the other side of the bed. "Do you need anything else?"

"No."

"I'll be in the living room. Shout if you need me."

But he already seemed to be out like a light. She left the bedroom slightly open so she could hear him if he called her. In the living room, she set the alarm on her phone so that she could check on him in two hours and plopped down on the sofa.

This was not how she had planned to

spend her evening, but given what had happened, there was nowhere else she'd rather be. She leaned back against the sofa and closed her eyes.

Next thing she knew, her cell phone alarm told her it had been a couple of hours and that she had to wake up John. She stood, her stiff muscles protesting. Stretching her arms up and out, she walked down the hall to John's bedroom.

He lay sound asleep on his side, just as she'd left him earlier. She stepped forward and observed he had long brown eyelashes that brushed his cheeks, which looked a little pink. Frowning, she put her hand to his forehead and thought he had a slight fever. She put a hand on his shoulder and tapped softly.

"What?"

"Do you know what day it is?"

"Sunday." He opened one eye and peered at her. "I'm fine."

"You're running a temp."

"I have a thick comforter over me, and it's the end of June." He pushed the covering away from him. "It's warm in here."

"I didn't know where to find a lighter blanket."

"I'm fine."

She frowned at him. "You're cranky."

"I got hit over the head, and it hurts. I deserve to be a little cranky."

She cocked her eyebrow at the word "little." He was a lot cranky in her book, since he was usually easygoing. It was too soon for more pain medication. Maybe he was hungry. "I can fix you some soup."

"No."

"Too hot for soup or you're not hungry?"

"I don't think I could keep it down."

"Saltines then? And some ginger ale?"

He buried himself in the pillow, and she reached over to move his hair away from his forehead. "You don't have to take care of me like that. I'm a grown man."

"Okay, okay. I'll be back."

In the kitchen, she opened every cupboard, trying to find crackers. He didn't seem to have much food, so she checked on him one more time before slipping out of the apartment and heading to the drugstore she'd seen across the street. Fifteen minutes later, she returned with saltines and Vernors, Michigan's answer for everything from tummy aches to nausea. She placed her purchases on the kitchen counter, then walked to the bedroom to see if John was okay.

The bedroom door was ajar, and she found that he had changed into the shorts and flung his jeans on the floor beside the bed. She picked them up and folded them before placing them on top of the dresser. At least he'd be more comfortable. She checked his forehead and noted it felt cooler. Good.

She returned to the living room. At loose ends, she turned on the large-screen television and settled on the couch to wait until it was time to wake up John again.

"JOHN, WAKE UP."

Reluctantly, he opened his eyes to find his personal tormentor standing over him. "Again?"

"Every two hours. What month is it?"

"June." He closed his eyes again. "See you in two hours."

Moments later, he heard his name again.

Groaning, he opened his eyes. "I thought you were going to let me sleep."

"It's been two hours. What day is it?"

"Is it after midnight?"

"It's almost four."

"Then it's Monday. Can I go back to sleep?"

He resumed his dream about trying to go through a room while being hit by wood planks. One hit him on the back of the head, and he sat up, gasping. Ugh, he shouldn't have done that so fast. It felt like ice picks had stabbed him in the nape of his neck and both eyes.

The bedroom door swung open, and light from the hallway spilled inside. "Are you okay, John? I heard you shouting."

"Just a dream." She leaned over and put her hand on his forehead. He reached up and put a hand over hers. "Really. I'm fine."

"It's time for more pain medication. And you need to take those antibiotics." She left the bedroom and returned moments later with a glass of water. She handed it to him and shook out the required tablets into her hand. "Here you go."

He hated being helpless. Hated having

to be looked after. He was an independent man who took care of himself. He didn't need her. But he swallowed the medication down.

She sat on the edge of the bed and looked at him. "How are you feeling?"

"Like I got hit in the head by something heavy."

She smiled. "Are you hungry? You haven't eaten anything since lunch. I'm not much of a cook but I saw you had makings for sandwiches."

He could use something to eat. "Did you get saltines?"

She stood. "I'll bring them to you."

He shook his head, but then winced at the pain. "No. I need to get up and move." He pushed the sheet off and carefully swung his legs to the side of the bed. She hovered around him as he stood, ready to catch him if he fell. But he stayed upright and took a few steps. "I can walk on my own, thanks."

"I'm here if you get dizzy."

Slowly, he was able to walk to the living room without any help, but the kitchen seemed so far away and he chose the couch instead. Cassie retrieved the box of crackers and pulled out one cellophane sleeve for him. She left and returned with two tall glasses of ginger ale with ice.

They sat on the sofa as she watched him eat a couple of saltines. "You don't have to keep such a close eye on me. I'm okay."

"Just making sure. I've never had to take care of anyone before."

"You take care of your dog."

"Evie is easy. Some kibble and water. Walks. And a belly rub before bedtime." She peered at him. "I've never had to actually look after another human being before."

"And what do you think?"

She shuddered. "I'd rather be mudding some drywall."

He grinned and ate another saltine. Cassie pointed the remote at the television. "Want to watch something?"

"Not much on at four in the morning."

"The local news is." She found the channel, and they settled in companionable silence as stories about vacation dos and don'ts and car insurance rates played out. The weather report said that the week would be hot but dry, which meant good news for the Buttuccis, who would be painting the house's exterior.

"The Belvedere Foundation is in the spotlight again as an assault at one of their contest homes occurred yesterday afternoon."

Both Cassie and John sat up and leaned forward. He was a news story? That hadn't happened before.

"Due to the incident, work on all houses will be suspended while the police investigation is being completed. A spokesperson for the Belvedere Foundation stated that they are adding more security measures to ensure the safety of all those involved in the project."

Cassie whistled. "This is definitely a twist no one had planned on."

"I'll call the brothers later to make sure they know about the update."

"I'm sorry."

She opened her eyes and looked at him. "Why are you apologizing?"

"If I hadn't been there, hadn't gone inside to investigate…"

"We'd still have a damaged house. And

it could have been worse. Maybe now the foundation will take security seriously."

He reached up and touched the back of his head.

"Careful. Don't mess with your stitches," she warned.

They'd had to shave off part of his hair to suture the wound, and he wondered how it looked. "Can you go get the hand mirror from my bathroom?"

"You want to check out their handiwork."

"Something like that."

She left the couch and returned with the requested mirror. Holding it at an angle, he tried to get the right position to see the back of his head. Finally, he gave up and laid the mirror on the sofa. Cassie joined him on the couch and tucked her feet underneath her. "Trust me. You don't want to see it."

He sighed and leaned his head back, but that made him feel dizzy, so he sat up once more. "I guess not."

"I have to tell you something, but I don't want you to get upset."

He turned to look at her, but she kept her gaze on the floor. "I got a call last night from Mr. Belvedere. They want us to meet him in his office this morning at ten." She glanced up at him. "Do you think he's going to fire us?"

"He can't fire someone that technically volunteered for the job in the first place."

"What if he says we're out of the contest?"

He reached out and put a hand on her knee. "It's not our fault that I got attacked. That someone is sabotaging our work."

"Right. But that's not the part that's going to make you upset."

He steeled himself for what she would say. "Okay. What else?"

"Your phone got a bunch of calls last night, and I might have told your mom you got hurt." She was biting her lip, clearly worried. "Are you going to kill me?"

The fact that his mother hadn't arrived at his apartment threatening to hurt the man who hurt her baby meant Cassie had defused the situation well. "What did you tell her?"

"That you got injured, but you were all right. And that I was watching over you so she didn't need to visit." She paused. "Did I handle that okay?"

His mom was probably delighted to hear that her bachelor son had a woman keeping an eye on him. At brunch the day before, she had been on his case about moving on after the end of his engagement. "You did great."

"I thought she was another reporter at first or I wouldn't have answered it."

He frowned. "Another reporter? How many called?"

She picked the phone up off the coffee table and handed it to him. "I lost track after seven. I told them all 'no comment.' Eventually I put it on silent because it wouldn't stop ringing, and I was worried it would wake you up."

"Thanks." He checked his call history and found a dozen missed calls and half as many voice mails. Closing his eyes for a moment, he realized how tired he still was despite sleeping most of the evening away. "I'll check them later."

She rose from her spot on the sofa and helped him lie down before bringing him a pillow. He wondered if he'd felt her lips pressed to his forehead before sleep overtook him.

CASSIE REQUIRED MORE than one carafe of coffee to make it through the rest of the day, she decided. After getting up every two hours to wake John, she felt as if she hadn't slept at all herself. She started a second pot of coffee since she knew they would both need the caffeine. John entered the kitchen, and she passed him his mug of coffee just the way he liked it. She'd found two travel mugs to take with them to the meeting with Belvedere. "We'll have to leave in a half hour."

He didn't respond as he took his first swallow of coffee.

They were meeting with the people at the Belvedere Foundation, and he'd need to change out of the shorts he'd put on last night. "Do you need help dressing?"

He stopped drinking long enough to look at her. "You're not helping me."

"You can't wear that for this meeting."

"What about you? You're wearing the same clothes as yesterday."

She looked down at the outfit she'd thrown on before heading to the house after John's call. "I don't have a choice. We don't have time to run by my house before the meeting."

"I might have something you could use."

"Your ex-girlfriend's clothes? That's not a good idea."

He crooked his finger, and she followed him into his bedroom, where he opened the closet doors and started to bring shirts out. He held a soft pink button-down one up to her. "It will be big enough on you to look like a dress. I'll give you a belt to cinch it in."

She slipped the shirt off the hanger and held it up to her body. "I'll have to roll the sleeves up, too. And it will only hit me midthigh, if I'm lucky."

"So keep your shorts on underneath. We can make it work."

"You've done this kind of thing before?"

"Hey, needs must." He pulled out a knit shirt for himself. "I don't think I could put on a tie today. Can you tie one?"

"Never tried. Are you sure you'll need one?"

"Good point."

She grinned. "Like you said, we can make it work."

She walked into his bathroom to change. She was swimming in the shirt, but maybe his belt would make a difference. Who would have thought that she would look almost fashionable? More so than she usually did anyway.

Dressed and caffeinated, Cassie drove them to the Belvedere Foundation's offices. When they walked inside the boardroom, she was surprised to see the other teams already there. "Guess we're not the only ones he called."

"Guess not."

She chose a chair and John took the one next to it. A number of the other contestants asked how he was, and Nick from the house next door approached him. "That was awful what happened to you yesterday."

John nodded. "I never saw who it was, unfortunately. Got hit from behind."

Nick shook his head. "Cowards. They need to do something before someone really gets hurt."

Like John hadn't been? She was about to say so to Nick when Mr. Belvedere began speaking. "If we could all take our seats, we can start this meeting." He waited until the din in the room faded away. "As you all have heard by now, John Robison was attacked in his contest house yesterday afternoon."

Eyes turned to look at John, and Cassie put a hand on his arm.

"Because of this incident and the sabotage that also happened, we are instituting new security measures."

"Because of the ongoing inspections, we are maintaining the open-door policy during the workday. However, we have hired a security firm to monitor the houses 24/7 starting today. They have lists of the contestants and approved workers, and anyone on the premises will be required to show ID when asked." Mr. Belvedere paused to look at everyone in the room. "There was talk about scrapping the contest altogether, but we have five families depending on all of you to finish what you have started. If anyone wants to quit, please do so now and you will be replaced immediately."

Cassie held her breath, waiting to see if anyone dropped out. Leave the contest now? No way. She'd see this through to the end, no matter what.

John said, "I'm still in. Cassie?"

"Me, too."

All the other teams also agreed to remain in the contest. Nick said, "They can't scare me away."

Mr. Belvedere smiled. "Good. I'll look forward to your next updates in a couple of weeks. There's not much time left until the judging." He paused before adding, "Mr. Robison and Ms. Lowman, if you two could stay behind for a few minutes."

John glanced at her with his eyebrows raised. Cassie shrugged. It felt like getting called out by the teacher to remain after class. Mr. Belvedere waited until the rest of the group had left before coming over to where they sat. He looked down at John. "I'm glad that the attack on you wasn't any more serious."

"Me, too."

Mr. Belvedere pulled out the chair next to John and took a seat. "The police were here earlier, asking about the two of you. I assured them that we had vetted you both completely before admitting you into the contest. Their concern, obviously, is that the sabotage has escalated into violence."

"The attacker didn't expect me to be there or to investigate the noise he was making."

"And you really didn't see who it was?"

"No, sir. I wish I had."

Mr. Belvedere put a hand on John's shoulder. "Unfortunately, this business is painting the good we're trying to do in a negative light. I'm counting on the new security measures to stop these attacks."

"My dog is better than any alarm system, so protective. I like having her on site."

Mr. Belvedere smirked at this. "Yes, I heard the plumbing inspector met her up close and personal."

"If he had listened to me before opening the door, he would have been fine." She crossed her arms over her chest. "So, just to clarify, are we out of the contest?"

Mr. Belvedere frowned. "No. We expect great work out of the both of you despite what's happened. Although the police won't release the work site back to you until next week."

Cassie calculated that this would put

them behind even more, and the timeline was already tight. But then, she'd worked to more stringent deadlines with her father and had brought the project in on time and on budget. She could do it again.

Mr. Belvedere thanked them for their determination and loyalty to the project. "I hope to meet with you later under better circumstances, but I know that the two of you are both tough competitors. This won't keep you down for long."

He left them then, saying he had to get to another meeting. Cassie turned to John. "Guess we get to play hooky from work."

He closed his eyes. "Good. I'm ready for a nap."

CHAPTER NINE

EVENTUALLY, WORK CONTINUED at the house without any further incidents. Cassie's next big job on her list was to install the shower pipe so that the Buttucci brothers could finish putting up the walls in the bathroom, then tile the shower and tub area. She'd debated on the best fixture and settled on a handheld shower so that could it be used at a lower level for washing the boys at bath time. John had agreed and found a deal on a nickel-plated set that had been a staple in homes during the 1950s.

Because of the six-foot height of the pipe for the showerhead, she couldn't reach where she needed to. She'd brought in a ladder, but with the sloped sides on the tub, it wouldn't fit where she needed it to be. Sometimes she hated her height.

She found John in the backyard, playing fetch with Evie. She hated to interrupt his playtime, but she needed a taller person's help. Spotting her at the back door, Evie bounded over with the ball in her mouth. Cassie grasped the ball and threw it to the far corner of the backyard. Evie raced after it as Cassie joined John. "Could you help me with something?"

"Sure."

He followed her inside to the bathroom. She held up the shower pipe. "I can't reach."

"Oh, right." He held the pipe in place and she got ready for the next step.

"Here, you'll need these," she said, and snapped a pair of goggles on him. "I've installed the pipes for the waterlines, but now I need to have this pipe that will come out of the wall and attach to the showerhead."

She put on goggles and then checked the connections. "We're going to attach the shower pipe, then sweat it and check for any leaks."

"Sweat?"

"Solder. It involves a propane torch to weld together the connections." She wiggled her eyebrows. "I have to admit that using the torch is my favorite part of the process."

He laughed and she noticed him shift his stance to get a stronger grip on the pipe. It brought her into even closer contact with him. "Sorry it's so tight in here," she said.

"I'm not complaining."

The joke warmed her, but the look in his eyes told her he was serious. She clamped a flame guard screen around the wood wall frame and then started the torch. With John standing so close to her, she carefully soldered the fittings to prevent any leaks. She couldn't quite reach the topmost section, so she handed the torch to John.

"You want to solder the joints together at the ell."

He followed her instructions and then asked, "Like this?"

"Yes, a little more." She handed him a rag and took the torch from him. "Now wipe off the excess solder." She nodded. "Good. Want to test it now?"

"You're the expert. Do you think it's safe?"

"It better be or my Daddy taught me wrong."

She left him to turn the water back on. When she returned, John had stepped out of the tub. With Cassie's approval, he then turned on the cold-water valve. A clunk and a hiss, and water poured out of the shower pipe. Cassie clapped her hands as John looked both surprised and pleased.

She turned off the valve and tested the one for hot water. They held their breath as water came out of the spout and flowed into the tub.

John held up his hand, and she gave him a high five. "Nice plumbing job, Mr. Robison."

"I only did what you told me to, Miss Lowman."

John kept a hold of her hand and she let him. She grinned and used her other hand to shut off the valve. "I'll call to let the inspector know the bath fittings are ready to be inspected, and then we can finish putting up the drywall and start the tiling in here."

"The house is really coming together."

"I love when it gets to this point. Seeing the frame and trying to imagine what the finished product will look like is hard. But this— This is fun. Thank you for your assistance."

John took a step closer to her and wiped her cheek with his free palm. "My pleasure."

She swallowed hard at his touch and kept her eyes on his. She remembered the kiss they'd shared before and wondered if it would be as good as the first time. Reaching up on tiptoe, she put her lips to his. He brought an arm around her back and nudged her closer so that they were pressed together. The kiss continued until someone else cleared their throat.

Cassie jerked back from John to find Biggie watching them from the doorway. He shook his finger, but smiled at them before he let Tiny inside. "I thought you were installing the shower."

"We were. It's finished," she told them.

Tiny's eyebrows were raised as if he wasn't convinced. He huffed, "And now we kiss each other to reward a job well done? Things have definitely changed without your father being around."

"Leave them be, Tiny," Biggie said, a warning lilt to his voice. He disappeared, pulling his brother along with him.

Cassie groaned and leaned her head on

John's chest. "Why did they have to catch us kissing? Of all things."

John stroked his hand on her cheek before kissing her again. "I like the idea of kissing you every time you do a good job."

Cassie started to say something, but she was interrupted by the sound of her cell phone ringing. She answered, "Lowman Construction."

"Cass."

Her father. She walked out into the hall, dropping the volume of her voice. "Where are you?"

"You're not alone."

"No."

She heard three tiny beeps and checked her phone to see that her father had hung up. Unsure if she was upset by that or by the fact that he'd reached out to her at all, she blew a loud puff and tucked the phone into her jeans pocket. Back in the bathroom, John seemed to be watching only her. She pasted a smile on her face. "Sorry about that. Where were we?"

He colored and put his hands in his pockets. "It's late, and I should get going if you don't need me any longer."

The truth was they hadn't needed him to help with the reno since he was the ideas man. But Cassie appreciated the fact that he wasn't worried about getting his hands dirty. "Right. Have a good night."

He moved past her, and she looked away. The moment had obviously been missed.

But then abruptly he turned back and put a hand on her cheek. He leaned in and she let her eyes close to revel in the kiss. "Now it's a good night," he whispered.

CASSIE PULLED UP in front of her mother's house and frowned at the sight of an unfamiliar car in the driveway. Maybe Andie had bought a new car? Or her mother had turned in hers for a smaller and cheaper model? She grabbed the bag from Lucille's off the passenger seat beside her and walked up to the front door, letting herself inside. The living room was empty. "Mother?"

No answer. She checked her watch—she was right on time for Sunday's family dinner. In the kitchen, she took the antipasto salad from the bag and laid it on the counter next to the stove, where a Bolognese sauce simmered. Her mother had to be in the house, since she wouldn't leave without turning off the burner.

Cassie strained to hear voices, but only silence filled the house. She folded the paper bag from Lucille's and stashed it with others under the kitchen sink. It was Sunday, right? She hadn't lost track of time again, had she? "Mother?"

The French doors that led to the backyard opened, and her mother entered, trailed by a woman in a pastel blue linen suit. "As you can see, I put a lot of time into my garden." Her mother spotted her standing there. "Oh, Cassandra, you're early." She turned back to the stranger. "This is my daughter, Cassandra. You might have heard she's in the Belvedere Foundation's contest."

The woman beamed. "Congratulations on the contest. I'm Selena, your mother's Realtor."

Realtor? The room seemed to sway for a moment, and Cassie put a hand on the counter to steady herself. "Nice to meet you."

Her mother gave the sauce a stir, then placed the wooden spoon on the spoon rest.

"Selena, let me show you the bedrooms so you can get those measurements."

The two women left the kitchen while Cassie tried to quell the tremors in her chest. Her mother talking about selling the house was very different from having an actual Realtor taking measurements. She collapsed on a stool. She'd never thought that the family home would be sold before she was married and had kids. She'd always imagined bringing her own family here for the holidays. Taking her children trick-or-treating in the neighborhood that she'd grown up in. Standing around the dining room table with hands clasped while they shared what they were thankful for. Sitting on the floor in the family room while unwrapping gifts by the Christmas tree. Egg hunts in the backyard while a ham baked in the oven.

"Didn't you get my message that dinner had to be pushed back an hour tonight?" Her mother's voice broke her reverie.

"No. I've been so busy that I haven't paid much attention to my phone."

"Except when your father calls." Her mother brushed past her and checked the sauce once more before turning to her. "Selena thinks the house will sell pretty quickly, depending on what we price it at. I could be moving by the end of the summer."

"I can't believe this. It's happening too fast."

"I've talked about this for months."

Her mother had, but Cassie had clung to the hope that nothing would have to change. That it would go away without having to go to such extremes. "Where will you go?"

"I haven't decided yet, but your aunt has offered to let me stay with her for a while."

Cassie glanced around the kitchen. "We're losing it all, aren't we? The house. The business."

Her mother put a hand on her shoulder. "But we'll still have each other. Our memories. That's more important than anything."

It wouldn't bring her father back, though. Cassie rubbed at her eyes. "I know. It's just…"

Selena entered the kitchen and held up her tablet. "I have all the figures I require. I'll start putting this into the system and have the listing contract ready for you to sign first thing tomorrow morning. Should I come back around nine?"

"That would be fine. I'll walk you to your car."

Her mom and the real estate agent left the kitchen as Andie entered and looked behind her. "Who was that with Mother?"

"Her Realtor."

Andie groaned and took a seat on the stool next to Cassie. "Isn't she jumping the gun a little?"

"That's what I thought, too." Cassie stood and walked to the stove to stir the sauce. "I didn't think this would ever happen."

"Because you've always been in denial about Daddy."

Cassie bristled at the accusation. "Because I defend him and want to believe the best about him?"

"Because you don't want to face the truth that your hero betrayed not only his clients and his family, but that he left you. His precious baby girl. That's what hurts you the most. That you're not so special to him after all."

"You've always been jealous of my relationship with Daddy."

"Well, you can have him. He's a thief. And a liar."

Cassie slammed the wooden spoon onto the counter, splattering red tomato sauce. Prickling with anger, she told her sister, "Take. That. Back."

Andie crossed her arms over her chest. "It's true. He stole from everybody, including us. The house is one more thing we have to lose because of his behavior. And the one who is suffering the most is Mother."

"Daddy wouldn't let that happen."

"He already has. I wish you'd wake up and realize the fact that he's not the man you thought he was."

Their mother arrived and chastised them both. "Girls, enough!"

Cassie retreated to the dining room and gripped the back of a chair for support, wishing for strength. She could hear her mother consoling Andie but didn't care. Let them talk. Let them figure it all out.

They couldn't talk away the hot anger that burned in Cassie's chest. Anger at her sister for saying such horrible things about their father. Anger at her mother for selling the house. But mostly, fury at her father. How could he do this to them? To her? He'd promised to be a good father and husband, but he'd left them to deal with this mess on their own.

Betrayed and abandoned by her father. She clutched the spindles until her knuckles turned white.

"Cassandra?" Her mother entered the dining room and stood behind her.

Cassie couldn't face her. Afraid that if she saw her mother's kind expression she'd crumple into tears. And she couldn't. Wouldn't. "Leave me alone."

"You need to apologize to your sister."

Cassie chuckled at the suggestion. "I'm not nine years old anymore where you can tell me what to do. You didn't hear what she said."

"You two were yelling loud enough for the neighbors to hear, so yes I did."

Cassie felt her mother put a hand on her shoulder, but she shrugged it off. "Please, don't touch me."

"Let's talk about this."

"What's there to talk about? You and Andromeda think Daddy's guilty, but I believe in him. I love him. And I can't stay here any longer and listen to the two of you."

"Just because I know he's guilty doesn't mean I don't love him."

But Cassie couldn't reconcile those two thoughts. *How could that be?* She started to walk out, but her mother called after her, "What about tonight's family dinner?"

Cassie paused in the doorway. "I'm not hungry." Then she left the house. Possibly forever.

JOHN TRIED TO take in all the positive changes that had been made to the house.

With the electrical and plumbing inspections complete, it was time to finish hanging the rest of the drywall. Cassie hired two extra hands to help finish the task. Once the drywall had been hung and other structural work finished, they would have to leave the house for a week so that it could set before they continued with the final stages.

John had made plans with Cassie to use

the time to find the rest of the supplies: paint, tiles, carpet and all the little things that turned a house into a home.

He stepped out of the way of one of the college students working with the drywall. He checked the garage for her, but she wasn't there. Tiny gave him an eye up and down before he returned to making marks on the drywall.

"Have you seen Cassie?"

"Depends. Why do you want to know?" Tiny asked, making another mark.

Because he wanted to know if what he was feeling was only one-sided or if she felt the same confusion over what seemed to be developing between. After that kiss. He wanted to ask her if she'd like to be friends outside of their professional relationship. Or more than friends, even. But instead of saying all of that to Tiny, he simply shrugged. "Just curious, I guess."

Tiny snickered. "Curious, huh? There are plenty of men curious about our Cassie. What are *your* intentions?"

Intentions? John felt as if the collar on his T-shirt had suddenly shrunk and was choking him. "Are you asking what I think you are?"

"Cassie acts like she's this tough cookie who can handle anything, but her feelings are as delicate as a cannoli shell. One bite, and she crumbles. Do you see what I'm saying?"

Maybe Tiny was right. He didn't need to complicate their professional relationship right now. They had to work together to complete the house and win the contest. Part of him protested that they could do that and pursue something more than friendship, but the rational side of him recognized that it would be prudent to wait. To hold off until later. "I'm not going to hurt her."

Tiny gave a harrumph and returned to his task. "She called me last night and said that she wasn't feeling well, but she hopes to be back tomorrow. Now make yourself useful and hand me that saw over there."

John handed him the requested tool. "Do you think you could teach me what you're doing there?"

"Measuring drywall? Sure." He made a pair of cuts, then handed the sheet to the other helper, who would deliver it to Biggie inside. "The trick is to measure once, cut twice."

John paused and peered at the man. "Don't you have that the other way around?"

"You want me to teach you or not?"

WITH THE DRYWALL COMPLETE, Cassie could see where they were heading. It had been a long day, so she'd sent everyone home but had stayed behind. She needed a moment to herself in this house before they had to leave it for a while to let the mud dry. With the walls complete, they could turn their focus to painting. It was finally all coming together.

She pulled a metal folding chair into the living room and sat looking out the front window, absently petting Evie who sat at her side. The neighborhood was quiet and calm. With the new security guards on site, they hadn't had any worries about problems with vandalism or intruders, but she appreciated the dog's presence all the same.

Evie whined, and Cassie leaned over to place a kiss on the dog's forehead. "I know. We'll go home soon for dinner. Mama just wants to sit for a moment and appreciate the soothing silence."

A noise from the kitchen perked up Evie, who gave a soft growl, and Cassie stood. She peered into the darkness and called out, "Show yourself before I sic my attack dog on you."

"You wouldn't hurt your old man, would you?" Her father stepped into the room but stayed back so that he wore the shadows of the room.

Evie trotted over to him, and he crouched to pet her. "You've been taking care of our girl? Protecting her?" Evie's tail thumped the floor.

Her father looked different than he had the last time Cassie had seen him. Almost twelve months had taken a toll. He was thinner. Paler. With a hint of sadness around his eyes. Part of her wanted to run to him and throw her arms around him. The other, logical, part made her stay where she was, wondering why he had shown up now. "What are you doing here?"

"Are we alone?"

She was sure he knew the answer to that

question. "You would've been watching the work site to make sure we were."

He nodded and stood to his full height. "Cass, I miss you and Andie and your mother."

"Then you should come home."

"You know what would happen if I did."

Yes, she did. But wouldn't it be better knowing he was in police custody, rather than worrying about where he was? "Why are you here?"

"I wanted to see your big project."

"There's a security guard outside."

"He's on a break and will be for..." he checked his watch "...another eleven minutes, so we don't have much time. Give me the grand tour."

She paused for a moment, then approached him, still unsure if she should hug him, although she certainly wanted to. He took the decision out of her hands and pulled her into an embrace. She closed her eyes as he held her tight and placed a kiss above her ear.

With moist eyes, she led him down the hallway to show him the bathroom. "I installed the copper piping just like you taught me. We're going to tile in the tub area with glass tiles."

"Glass tiles? They cost a lot more than ceramic."

"But they'll make a bigger impact on the overall design."

He looked closely at the pipes. "The joints should be further apart to allow more flow. I thought I taught you better."

She stepped back from him, upset at his criticism. "I have so much to ask you."

"Another time."

There couldn't be another time. As it was, she'd have to call the detective once her father left. They'd probably put more surveillance on her and her family. "I don't want to believe you did what they say you did, so please tell me. Did you take that money?"

Her father swallowed and looked deep into her eyes. "Don't ask me to tell you something you don't want to know."

A crack in her heart seemed to widen, and she put a hand to her chest. "You need to turn yourself in, Daddy. You need to face up to what you did."

"I can't go to prison."

She took a step further away from him. "You don't understand what your abandoning us has done to Mother. She has to sell the business, the house."

"Stop."

Her father hurried past her. Cassie was close behind him. "Please, Daddy. This is tearing apart our family. Come home."

He turned back to look at her. "I have to go." He headed for the kitchen, and a moment later, she heard the back door close.

Cassie felt her legs fold, and she sat on the living room floor, staring into the darkness. She let the tears fall down her face for a few minutes before she pulled her cell phone from her jeans pocket and dialed her mother's number.

Her mother met her at the front door of the family home when she arrived with Evie in tow. Cassie asked, "Did you call the detective?"

"He's on his way here." Her mother stepped back to allow her room to enter. "Put the dog in the kitchen. I've got leftover chicken she can eat if she's hungry."

"She's always hungry, Mother."

They walked into the kitchen, where the

cooking scents of dinner still lingered. Her mother pulled out a plastic container from the refrigerator and set it on the counter. "How did he look?"

Cassie watched her take meat off the bones and place it in a bowl. "Tired. Sad."

Her mother nodded and put the bowl on the floor where Evie wolfed down the chicken. When she stood up again and looked at Cassie, she could see the red rims around her mother's eyes. "He was okay, though."

"What did he say?"

"That he misses us, but he can't come home."

Her mother wrapped her arms around her and Cassie felt as if she never wanted to let go. She did, eventually, and her mom led her into the living room. "He calls you. He visits you. And not one word to me."

"I'm sorry, Mother."

Her mother turned from the window to look at her. "It's not your fault that he can't face me. He knows that I wouldn't let him sweet-talk me into forgiving him."

"He didn't ask for forgiveness."

"Just as well." She sat on the love seat, her legs crossed at the ankles. "I'd already forgiven him for ignoring me while he pursued bigger and better projects. Convinced each was going to be the one that would make him rich. Famous. Known."

"He was providing for us."

"Cassandra, I'd rather have had him home with us instead of a fatter savings account."

She remembered well the nights and weekends her father would be on a work site rather than with them. Part of the reason she had started going to work with him was to spend time in his presence, even if she was sawing wood or mudding drywall.

There was a knock on the front door and her mother rose to answer it. She ushered George August into the living room. "Detective, I'm glad you could meet with us here. Can I get you something to drink?"

Even while being questioned by a detective, her mother never forgot how to be the ultimate hostess. Once the detective had a glass of freshly squeezed lemonade, he settled on the sofa while she and her mother squeezed together on the love seat. He took a long sip of lemonade and placed the sweating glass on the coaster her mother had provided. "Thank you, Mrs. Lowman. That reminds me of the lemonade my grandmother used to make."

"Can we just get this over with, please?" Cassie didn't look forward to being grilled, even if she didn't have much to say. "You know my father came to see me tonight."

"Yes, I questioned the security guard that was on duty at the time. He says he didn't see anything."

"My father's not stupid. He wouldn't have walked into a trap."

Her mother put her hand on Cassie's. The detective pulled out a notebook and pen. "Why don't you tell me what happened?"

Cassie recounted the events of the evening. "I asked him to turn himself in, but he's afraid."

Detective August looked up at her, pausing his writing. "He told you he's afraid?"

"No. But I can see what this is doing to him. He's lost weight, so he's not eating.

And he's not sleeping, if the bags under his eyes are any indication." She glanced at her mother. "I tried to tell him about how you're selling the business and the house, but he couldn't listen to that. I'm sorry."

Her mother patted her hand. "Don't you apologize for him."

Cassie turned back to the detective. "He wouldn't admit to anything. Even when I asked him to tell me what he'd done."

"That's not surprising," the detective said. "He never has admitted to anything."

At this, her mother narrowed her eyes at him. "Have you questioned my husband before about your suspicion that he was embezzling from his company?"

"I'm not at liberty to say."

Her mother leaned forward. "What you're not saying speaks louder than what you are."

The detective cleared his throat. "Uh, Cassie. What else can you tell me? Did he say where he's been hiding?"

"No."

"Did he say he would be in touch again?"

Her mother looked at her. Cassie shook her head. "No."

"What did he say?"

"That I was wasting money by using glass tiles rather than ceramic. And that I had installed the copper pipes too close together."

Her mother briefly smiled, then went to stare out the window. Cassie sighed and held out her hands, pleading. "He wasn't there more than ten minutes. How much could he say in that time?"

"You'd be surprised." The detective took the glass of lemonade and gulped the rest of it down, then stood. "I shouldn't have to repeat this, but if he contacts either one of you again, you need to let me know immediately."

"We understand." Her mother led him out. "Thank you for coming, Detective."

"Thank you for the lemonade."

Her mom returned and sat beside Cassie. "Glass tiles?"

Cassie gave a shrug. "They're pretty. And they fit with John's vision."

Her mother leaned over and put her

hands gently on Cassie's face. "You're be-coming your own woman, Cassandra."

If that was what glass tiles meant, then Cassie would take it.

CHAPTER TEN

"ANDROMEDA, WHAT ARE you doing here?" Cassie stepped off the ladder and put her paintbrush in the tray. She hadn't seen her sister since the evening the real estate agent had visited their mom's place.

"I can't stop in to see how things are coming along?" Andie glanced around the living room. "Where's Evie?"

"In the backyard chasing squirrels."

"Oh, good."

Cassie glanced at her sister's outfit and wondered why her sister would arrive at a construction site in a white linen sundress and two-inch heels. True, she was probably on a break from work, as a receptionist for a doctor's office, but the house wasn't exactly clean and spotless. And her dog had a penchant for jumping on Andromeda to reach her face and give doggy kisses.

"Do you know if we're out of this white

paint for the trim?" John asked from the hallway.

Andie turned toward him and gave him a long once-over, a smile playing around her lips. So that was the real reason why she had come dressed to impress. "Cassie, aren't you going to introduce me?"

Cassie gestured at her. "John, this is my older sister, Andromeda. Andromeda, this is John, the designer on the project."

John gave a short nod to her and held up the small can of white paint. "So, do we have any more of this or not?"

"Tiny had some in one of the twins' rooms."

"Thanks." He looked over at her sister, and Cassie was prepared for him to linger at Andie's side, but he did the opposite. "Nice to meet you," he said and disappeared into a bedroom.

Andie frowned at Cassie. "What was that about? He barely looked at me."

Her gorgeous sister was used to men ogling her when they first met her. Cassie doubted Andromeda had ever been ignored by a man before. She didn't know why John's reaction gave her an odd thrill, but it did. "He's too busy painting to stop and admire you."

Andie waggled a finger at her. "Whatever. Are you going to show me the rest of the place?"

Cassie looked her sister over again. "We're in the middle of painting. Are you sure you want to walk through wearing white?"

"I visited Daddy before at his work sites without a problem, so I think I'll be fine." She stepped up to the replacement kitchen cabinets that were stacked in the living room until Cassie had finished painting. She ran a hand along the surface. "I love the wood on these."

"We do, too." She cocked her head toward the kitchen. "There's more." She pointed out the window seat. "Dining over there. I found a cool stained glass chandelier to put above the table."

"Stained glass?"

Cassie had forgotten that her sister's master's thesis for art history had been the history of stained glass art in Detroit-area churches. "It's in a box over here. Come see."

Andromeda gave a murmur of appreciation as Cassie lifted the light fixture from its protective wrapping. "Gorgeous work. Probably from the 1920s. Where did you find it?"

"Architectural salvage warehouse."

Andromeda glanced around the room and nodded. "Those yellow walls and the southern light coming in from the window will make the glass gleam like jewels. Good work."

"Thanks."

Buoyed by her sister's compliment, she showed her the rest of the house. Andie loitered in the master bedroom where John painted the white trim along the ceiling. She crossed her arms over her chest and gave a nod. "I love what you're doing in here."

John dabbed more paint on to the trim. "It's gray walls with white trim."

"Tell me about your vision for this room."

"Your sister can tell you."

"But it's your vision, John."

He stopped painting but didn't come down off the ladder. "Lavender with navy accents. I'm using an old door to create a headboard. Thick comforter with lots of pillows. Everything soft and plush. This will be the parents' retreat after a long day of jobs and kids."

"It's great."

John returned to his painting, and Cassie ushered her sister to one of the bedrooms they were decorating for the twins. "John's going with a garage theme for the kids' rooms."

Andromeda frowned. "Garage?"

"The boys like cars and trucks, so we're making it look like a mechanic's garage. A huge case where they can line up their cars. A workbench with toy tools. And we're putting in black-and-white carpet tiles. Bold primary colors for the walls."

"Hey, sweetie." Tiny put his can of paint down on the floor and came over to her sister to kiss Andromeda's cheeks. "How're you doing?"

"Oh, you know me, Tiny. Still looking for a job that I can actually use my degree for. But I can't complain. Dr. Frazier pays me well to be her receptionist."

"You'll get that job one day. Nothing keeps you Lowman women down."

"Thanks." She nodded toward the doorway. "So what's the story on your designer over there?"

Tiny chuckled and then let out a long sigh. "He's coming along. Pretty bright guy, but he's got a ways to go before he's on par with your sister."

Andromeda put a hand on his shoulder. "Where's your brother? I don't want to leave without saying goodbye."

"Media room next door. Got to get this painting done."

"My sister's favorite part of the job."

Cassie wrinkled her nose at the lie. Her dad had often teased her about how much she disliked painting. She liked it when the task was completed, but the process of doing it gave her headaches from more than the paint fumes. She didn't have the hand for fine work that Tiny and Biggie had. They could paint straight lines without using painter's tape. They didn't have drips or smudges or mistakes like she did. Even John had proved to be a master painter. She didn't mind leaving them the task.

Andromeda popped into the next room. Biggie dropped his supplies down and wrapped her in his arms, lifting her off the floor. She squealed with laughter until he put her back on her feet. "How I've missed you, Biggie." Andie gave him a smack on his lips.

"Miss Andie, you're a sight for sore eyes. Gorgeous as ever."

"Flattery like that will get you everywhere." She put her hands on both his cheeks and kissed him again. "If you were twenty years younger, I'd marry you in a heartbeat."

Biggie blushed and stared at the floor. "Miss Andie."

"You're going to give the poor guy heart palpitations." Cassie linked her arm through her sister's and pulled her into the living room. "So that's the house."

"I'm glad you hired the brothers on this project. With Daddy's company gone, I bet most of their work had dried up."

"This contest means as much to them as it does to me. With my half of the prize money, I can restart Lowman Construction and give them steady jobs again."

Andie leaned down to test the wood floor. "I can see touches of Daddy in what you're doing here, but there's more of you emerging in the design."

Cassie shook her head. "Not me. John."

Andie stood and looked into Cassie's eyes. "Don't sell yourself short like that, Cass. Before, you always gave Daddy the credit. Now it's John? How about realizing that you bring just as much to the project as them?"

Did she do that? Without realizing it, maybe she had. But it was her effort that had gotten her into the contest. And it was going to be her effort that won it, as well. "You're right. I'm not just Daddy's helper anymore."

"Exactly."

The two sisters looked at each other for a long moment. Cassie cleared her throat. "About that fight..."

Andie held up her hand, stopping her apology. "We were both upset about Daddy, and we said some things we shouldn't have."

"Still, I'm sorry."

"Me, too." Andie grinned at her warmly. "Well, gotta get back to scheduling appointments and filing. Walk me to my car?"

At the curb, Andromeda opened the car door but turned back to look at the house. "Mom told me that Daddy visited you."

Cassie nodded but didn't know what else to say. Why had he chosen her to be the one he'd visit? Was it because he thought they were closer and as such she wouldn't say anything? Had it been the house that he was really visiting? She could see the hurt in her sister's eyes. "Yes, he did."

"Did he ask about me?"

"He said he missed you." Andie gave a nod, but Cassie could see that those few words weren't enough. "I told him that he needed to turn himself in."

Andie burst out with a laugh and flicked her hair to one side. "Like Daddy would ever admit that he did something wrong." She quickly added, "I'm not trying to get into another fight. We both believe what we do about Daddy, but I'm sorry we let that get between us."

Cassie looked down at the ground. "I might have been wrong about him. And it hurts to realize that."

Andie put a hand on her shoulder. "I don't want to lose you, too, Cassie."

Cassie smiled. "Me, either."

Then Andie was hugging her. "Good. Let's do dinner one night soon. And you can tell me more about your designer." She got in her car and leaned out the open window. "If I were you, I'd ask John out. He's clearly interested in you."

Cassie almost choked at the suggestion. "Are you kidding me? We're just working on this project together, and we need to keep it professional."

"Cass, when a man doesn't give me a second look but only has eyes for you, he's obviously hung up on you. Professional or not."

Cassie waved as her sister drove off, but the words she'd said remained stuck in her mind long after.

LUNCH EATEN, JOHN could feel lethargy setting in as he sat in the backyard, leaning against the tree and petting Evie, who had eaten his pizza crusts. If only he could close his eyes for just a moment…

"Ready to get back to work?" Cassie asked.

He opened one eye and peered at her standing over him. "We can't rest another five minutes?"

"I want to finish painting the rooms so we can start on the kitchen. That's going to eat up a lot of our time. And our budget."

He groaned but still sat on the ground, his fingers buried in the dog's thick fur. "Five minutes won't kill us, Cassie."

She sighed and dropped to sit between them. "So what did you think of my sister?"

He'd been focused on painting and hadn't really thought about her much. But Cassie wanted his impression. "She's okay."

"Okay? My sister is gorgeous. Everyone knows that she's the pretty one."

Cassie wore her usual worn T-shirt and jeans with rips and stains, her hair pulled back into a messy knot on top of her head. Even so, she looked more appealing to him than her sister had. "Don't underestimate yourself. You're just as pretty."

Cassie snorted. "You really do need to

rest if you believe that. Exhaustion and heat must be playing games with your eyes."

"My eyes are fine."

"Andromeda competed for Miss Michigan. How can I possibly compare?"

"I'd love to draw you sometime." John scooted a little closer to her and pushed a wayward strand of hair off her forehead. "You have the most expressive eyes I've seen. They're the color of good bourbon, which makes me want to drink you up."

Cassie swallowed but didn't move away. "Really?"

"Yes." He dropped his hand. What was he doing? He'd been thinking about kissing her when he had decided that they needed to keep it professional.

"Are you two planning on wasting the afternoon playing kissy-face or are we getting back to work?" Tiny called from the back door.

Cassie shot to her feet. "Be right there." She didn't look at him as she asked, "Are we playing kissy-face?"

John stood, wondering what it would be like to spend the rest of the afternoon kissing her. Instead he took a deep breath and shook his head. "Probably not a good idea."

The light in her eyes dimmed a little, and he immediately regretted his words.

"Right. Probably not," she agreed and rushed back to the house.

Evie looked up at him, and he rubbed her head. "What am I going to do, girl?"

But the dog didn't seem to have any answers. John knew what he needed to do. Keep his head down. Keep working. And try to forget the way the sun had brought out those golden highlights in Cassie's dark brown hair and made her skin glow.

THE END OF July brought another meeting at the Belvedere building. Cassie hated taking even a morning off to sit in a boardroom and talk. She'd rather be busy laying the living room floor, or paint the entire house again, if it meant avoiding another meeting. She'd even give up her precious coffee to go back to work.

After twenty minutes of talking that got them nowhere, she softly groaned and threw her head back. Next to her, John smirked and whispered, "We should be done soon, and you can go back to your sawdust."

"Promises, promises. We have three weeks left. Three." She looked down the table at Mr. Belvedere, who had chosen to wear a purple bow tie. "What did we learn that he couldn't have put into an email?"

"And finally, the promised next twist in the contest."

She sat up and waited for the shoe to drop. What monkey wrench was he about to throw into their plans? She had posted a countdown in the mudroom of deadlines that would take them up to August twentieth and the end of the contest. There was no wiggle room for twists.

"As you know this contest is part of the larger city and community efforts to refresh the neighborhood, and that includes public and outdoor spaces. Therefore, we will be pairing each team with a landscaper to create a plan for the front yard and back of each house." Mr. Belvedere smiled wider. "We want the living space outside to be as creative and useful as the inside."

Cassie groaned again and put her head down on the table. "Oh, come on."

John leaned closer to her. "What's so bad about creating a landscape plan? We were going to cut the grass and tidy up the front and back anyway."

"Where am I going to fit a landscaper into my schedule?"

"Yes, I've seen that you haven't left much room for anything else in the schedule. Not even sleep."

"And what about if the landscaper has wild ideas that don't fit with what we've designed?"

"Well, let's not create more problems where there aren't any. At least, right now."

John was clearly doing his best to stifle a laugh. She didn't know whether to holler at him or laugh along with him. His smile was sweet and almost convincing.

Mr. Belvedere announced the meeting was over and Cassie dragged herself to her feet. She was tired. Exhausted. Long hours painting had left her feeling cranky and out of sorts. And now she had to find extra hours in a day that held only twenty-four.

JOHN SAT ON the front porch and stewed. The landscaper had agreed to meet him almost an hour ago, and still there was no sign of him. But then, this was the third appointment he'd made with the man who had canceled the last two times. It didn't take an MBA to know this was no way for a person to run a business.

He got out his cell phone and called the landscaper's phone number. It rang once and moved him straight to voice mail. He waited for the customary beep. "Mr. Crosby, I'm calling to inform you that you are fired from this job. We no longer require your services."

He hung up and put his phone back in his pocket. Great. What was he going to do now? Inside the house, Cassie was laying the tongue and groove hardwood floor in the living room. He stopped at the unfinished edge. "I fired the landscaper."

She glanced up at him and wiped her forehead with the back of her hand. "I can't deal with it right now, John. I've got to get this floor down so we can start the kitchen."

"So don't deal with it. Leave me to find our own landscaper while you get the house finished. Whoever it is has to be better than the joker they paired us with."

"Uh, are you sure? Biggie or Tiny could—"

"Yes, I'm sure. I've already had some ideas on how to use the exterior of the house to our advantage. Close your eyes and imagine the backyard as it is. I've planned a vegetable garden on the far left side. Now imagine a wooden swing set for the boys closer to the house. Or maybe put a tire swing in that tree. Patio with a table where the Tanners could eat outside summer evenings."

"That's the backyard. And in the front?"

John pursed his lips. "I haven't thought that far ahead. But that's where a landscaper would come in handy. I've got a buddy who just had his house built last year. I'll call and see who he worked with."

Cassie sat back on her heels. "Actually, I know someone who would be willing to help us. And I'm sure she'd give us a deal that would be hard to refuse."

The idea intrigued him. "Really. Who?"

JOHN SAT ACROSS the dining room table from Cassie's mother, Lillian. She reminded him of one of those esteemed British actresses, with her clear blue eyes, pale skin and blond hair that had started to go white. Her imperious attitude helped foster that image as well. She folded her hands and placed them on the table. "Cassandra tells me that you need help with landscaping the house."

"Yes, ma'am." Not knowing what else to do, he grabbed his glass of iced tea and sipped it.

As she watched him, he realized that Cassie must take after her father, whom he had seen pictures of but never met. Her sister looked more like her mother, though Andromeda's darker coloring probably came from her father, Hugh. He'd love to sketch Lillian Lowman, and his fingers twitched with the need to hold a pencil and draw.

Finally, Lillian motioned for him to follow her. "I'll show you what I've done here. Maybe you can get some ideas from that."

He felt as if he'd disappointed her somehow, but he rose from his seat and followed her out to the kitchen and beyond to the backyard, where flowers bloomed still in the August heat. She had placed a broad-brimmed hat on her head as she moved among the plants, checking for weeds and testing the soil. "Cassandra mentioned that the family who will get your house has children. You'll want to stick with plants that are hardy and can stand up to trampling and rough play. No roses because of the thorns. And nothing toxic." She turned back to look at him. "Allocate a space for them where they can play. Cassandra mentioned a tree swing?"

"Yes, ma'am. I had one growing up at my grandparents' house."

"What about a tree house?"

"They're a little young yet to be climbing a tree."

"Then how about a playhouse they can also use to keep their toys and other outdoor things in?"

He visualized the backyard. "That could work. And even give them their own garden tools there to help their mom."

"Describe the front yard."

"Better yet, let me take you there."

She shook her head. "No, I'm not welcome on the work site."

"Says who? I'm inviting you."

Lillian sighed and adjusted her hat. "Cassandra's father was adamant that I was not to come to one of his projects."

"Well, Mr. Lowman isn't working on this house. And if I say you're welcome, then you are." He looked back at her, allowing no excuses. "Besides, he's not there."

Lillian had a coughing fit and seemed to color. Curious about her reaction but saying nothing, he convinced her to ride with him to the house. When they got to the site, she smiled warmly as she looked out the front windshield. "Yes. It's perfect."

She got out of the car before he did and walked up to the shrubs that stood guard over each side of the front door, fingering the leaves and frowning. "These have to go. They suck up too much water, and they're toxic to any cats in the neighborhood. You could tear them out and extend a covered porch where the family could sit on warm evenings." She walked further and put a hand on the brick exterior. "I can see that the Buttuccis painted this a lighter color. It evens out the variations of brick that's been used to repair and brightens up the front."

John asked, "What about plants?"

"Once the porch is built, you can plant some perennials that bloom at different seasons. Tulips and daffodils for spring. Some hibiscus for summer. Mums in the fall. And keep your colors similar. I'd go with yellows and oranges. Maybe red for the tulips."

The front door opened, and Tiny stepped out. "Lily?"

She turned and smiled at the man who jumped off the porch and engulfed her in a hug. "How long has it been?"

"The Christmas open house almost two years ago. I made you your favorite panettone with the raisins soaked in rum."

Tiny chuckled and kissed his fingertips. "This woman bakes a cake that makes angels weep." He winked at Lillian. "Does Cassie know you're here?"

"It was a spur-of-the-moment decision."

"I'll give you a personal tour." He held out his arm, which Lillian accepted, and they entered the house.

Cassie walked out of the house shortly after. She looked to him. "How did it go?"

"Good, I think. She's got a lot of great ideas."

She smiled. "I knew she would."

"Why didn't your dad let her work on his projects?"

Cassie shrugged. "He never thought about curb appeal beyond the exterior of the house. He dismissed Mother's ideas as spending money he didn't have."

"He missed out, then."

She glanced up at the house. "Yes. I guess so."

"I know so. She's going to make us the envy of the neighborhood. Just you wait."

CASSIE GROANED AND put a hand at the base of her spine. A long, hot bath sounded marvelous to her aching muscles, but she still had hours of work left before she could leave for the day. Her cell phone buzzed, and she grabbed it from her jeans pocket. "Lowman Construction."

"You need to find a new name. Otherwise, they'll associate you with everything I did."

She glanced around and quickly stepped outside to the backyard. "So now you'll admit it?"

"I didn't call you for that."

"You know you need to turn yourself in."

A pause. "I definitely didn't call to debate that."

"So why did you call, Daddy?"

"Something you said about the sabotage has been bugging me."

Her father called to talk about the vandalism? She shook her head. "It doesn't matter. It hasn't happened since John got hurt. Must have scared him off."

"Listen, I had this competitor years ago who liked to ruin my work with spray paint and filling the house with garbage. Thought it gave him a better chance at getting jobs and new clients. But all it did was make him look bad. Others in the business heard about it." He sighed on the other end. "Maybe I'm wrong, but it feels really similar."

She didn't think it was irrelevant. "Who was that competitor?"

"Doesn't matter. He died years ago."

She hung on to the phone, unsure of why he had called then. Was it to say something more? She suspected so. "Daddy, why do you keep calling me? Mother misses you and would love to talk to you."

"I'm sure she doesn't."

"But she does. And Andromeda—"

"Stop."

His tone was so forceful that it almost made her drop the phone. "Please come home."

"And face a possible prison sentence? I don't think so."

"Daddy—"

"I've already been on this phone call too long. Goodbye."

And then he was gone. Cassie stared at the cell phone and brought it to her forehead. Biggie stood nearby, watching her. She placed the phone in her pocket and retreated toward the house. "Best get back to work."

In the kitchen, she carefully stepped up the ladder. Biggie had followed and now handed her the stained glass dome that would hang above the kitchen table. She fastened it to the chain and the light bulb, then released it with a held breath. The chain should be able to hold the weight of the light fixture if her calculations were correct, but there was always that moment of doubt. But it held.

Biggie snapped the light on, and they both smiled at how it shot pretty shards of light in the sunny kitchen.

She came down from the ladder and turned to Biggie. "Did you ever know a competitor of Dad's that would sabotage his work?"

The man paused, then nodded slowly.

"I guess he's dead, but does anything about the sabotage we've faced remind you of him?"

Biggie didn't say a word but turned on his heel and left the room. Well, she guessed that answered that question. She folded the ladder and propped it against a blank wall and surveyed the kitchen. The last inspections were slated to happen soon; then John would decorate it for the judges' review next week. Only days left, and still so much to do.

She sighed and put thoughts of sabotage out of her mind so that she could concentrate on what was most important: the final result.

CHAPTER ELEVEN

THE HEAT OF mid-August would not let up, and tempers got shorter the higher the temperature rose. Cassie had taken to eating her lunch alone under the tree in the backyard so she wouldn't have to play referee between the brothers, who could fight over who had more pepperonis on their slice of pizza. Or who could paint a straighter line. She didn't care who was better. She wanted this project completed. The final inspection was tomorrow, and she had a list that was four pages long of items still to be completed.

Evie nuzzled beside her, and Cassie fed her a pizza crust, then buried her hand in the dog's thick fur. "You won't drive me crazy, will you, baby?"

John turned from the vegetable garden, where he was using a hoe to turn over the earth. "I promise you I won't."

"I was talking to Evie."

He smiled at her, making her heart skip a beat. "I know."

Cassie got up and walked to the edge of the garden. "It's too bad the Tanners won't be able to enjoy the fruits of your labors this summer."

"They will be next year. Loretta gave me a list of things they'll need to plant in the spring." He leaned on the hoe. "If I ever buy a house, I'm definitely putting in a garden."

"Why do you live in an apartment?"

"Thought I'd buy a house when I got married, but that never happened."

"Why didn't you get married? You're good-looking. You're talented. Kind. Funny."

"Well, as I told you, I was engaged, but she left shortly after I got laid off. And any plans I had for buying a house left with her."

Cassie winced. "Oh. Right. I'm sorry."

"I'm not. I don't want someone who's going to run at the first sign of trouble." He attacked the ground with a little more energy. "I don't know any marriage that hasn't had their share of troubles. Do you?"

"My parents had their issues, but I always thought they had a good marriage. But now I'm not so sure. My dad is one of those who run away, rather than sticking it out and dealing with the problem."

"I'm sorry, Cassie."

"Don't be. I made a hero out of my dad, but it turns out it's my mother that's the strong one. Who doesn't flinch at any trial but faces it with grace and dignity." She wrapped her arms around her middle. She'd really shortchanged her mom all these years. She'd been so wrong. Regret clogged her throat, and she swallowed. "I better get back to work."

"Did you ever tell your mom that?"

Cassie could never admit when her mother had been right. Maybe she was like her dad. "No."

"She might like to hear you share that with her. Just saying." He gave her a nod, then returned to his work.

Cassie headed to the house but turned back to look at him. "I'm almost done with my part. Tomorrow it's up to you. I expect you to win us this contest with your ideas."

He stopped hoeing and blinked several times. "Our ideas."

She gave him a short nod. "Our ideas."

She only hoped they'd be successful.

AT THE KNOCK on the front door, John took a deep breath. Well, here went nothing. Cassie opened the door and welcomed the plumbing inspector. "Mr. Daniels."

The inspector glanced anxiously around the living room. "My colleague mentioned a dog?"

John saw Cassie squelch a smirk before she answered, "I left her at home today since I knew you were going to be here."

Mr. Daniels gave a sigh of relief. "I'll look around and we'll go over my notes when I'm finished." When they started to follow him, Daniels held up his hand to stop them. "I'll do this alone."

"I was going to answer any questions you might have," she said.

"We'll leave it for the end."

Cassie raised her eyebrows at John. He gave her a skeptical look and walked out on to the newly constructed front porch, where he took a seat on the top step.

Cassie soon joined him and patted his shoulder. "Remember, he'll have a list of things we need to fix before giving us the certificate of occupancy."

"But—"

"They always come back with something. I think they believe they're not doing their jobs if they don't find at least three things to change. I've been through this many times before, relax."

He was glad for her expertise. If it hadn't been for her, he couldn't imagine how they'd have come as far as they had.

He stopped short at that thought. He'd started this contest wishing that he'd been paired with anyone but her, and he recognized he wouldn't be the improved designer that he was now if he'd had someone else. She'd listened and challenged him. Encouraged him. Taken his ideas and made them better. Then he'd tweaked it until it was perfection. They made an amazing team.

He opened his mouth to say something when a Detroit Police car pulled up to the curb and parked. Cassie frowned and stood, approaching the two police officers who got out of the vehicle. Another car pulled up, and Detective Tyler Matthews joined them. The detective asked, "Cassie, do you know where the Buttucci brothers are?"

John moved to stand shoulder to shoulder with her. "They were in the garage the last time I saw them. Are they in trouble?"

"No. Not at all," Matthews said. He addressed the officers and pointed to the house next door. "You'll find him over there. I'll join you after I thank the brothers."

Cassie glanced at John, but he had no explanation, either. He and Cassie both followed the detective to the garage. The sliding door was up, allowing a view of Tiny and Biggie, who were hanging tools on the corkboard above the carpenter's bench. Detective Matthews rapped on the garage wall. "Thank you both for your information. They're arresting the culprit right now."

Cassie looked as shocked as John felt. "Who is it?" he asked.

The detective motioned with his head to the neighboring house. "Nick Butler."

John thought about the attack. "He's the right height for the person who attacked me."

"He was also an employee of Luke Manchester, an old competitor of your father's. But I'll let the Buttuccis tell you that story." He gave the brothers a salute, then he was gone.

Cassie turned to Tiny and Biggie. "The sabotage from before?"

Biggie nodded as Tiny said, "You were right, Cassie. It was similar to what had happened. Down to the spray paint and spreading the garbage. Once we remembered, we knew it had to be someone associated with Manchester." He looked at John. "Though he never hurt anyone before."

"Not so glad to have been the first." John put a hand to where he'd been hit. It still ached sometimes.

"We did some digging and found Nick's connection to Manchester before he and his brothers started their own company. Then went to the police with what we knew."

John could see tears filling Cassie's eyes. "I'm sorry for not being more loyal. A better friend. I didn't really think that it was you two who did it."

Biggie took a step toward her. "We

know. But the fact that you could doubt us nearly killed us."

She slipped a hand into Biggie's. "Forgive me?"

The two brothers engulfed her in their arms, pulling her close as she kept apologizing. John felt like an intruder in an intimate moment but stood transfixed. These two tough, burly men let their tears fall unapologetically as they embraced their girl.

Someone cleared their throat behind them. John saw the plumbing inspector, who handed him a sheet of paper. "I'll be back in two hours to check these last couple items, but you've passed. I'll let the committee know."

John nodded and glanced at the two notations and smiled. He held the piece of paper up for them all to see. "We've passed!"

The brothers chuckled as they wiped their faces on bandannas yanked from their back pockets.

JOHN MET CASSIE in front of the house early Saturday morning. The back seat of his car was packed with all the items he'd been purchasing as he waited for this day. This would be only the first trip of many back to his apartment to retrieve the rest of the items. Some would work in the final design while others would have to be discarded. Kept for perhaps a future project. He wondered if that future would include Cassie.

They expected the furniture delivery truck at eight, so they had a moment before the chaos started. Cassie held out a cup of coffee to him. "You ready for this?"

He took a deep breath and tried to smile. That was the big question. Would they be ready for it to be all over? Then to face the judges and the Tanner family?

"Nick pleaded guilty to all charges," she told him. "Him and his design partner, Tiffany. Though it was Nick who beaned you on the head."

John rubbed the spot. "I wonder what'll happen to their house? And the family who was supposed to live there?"

"Yeah. I don't know. But it's not our problem." She nodded at the curb, where the delivery truck had stopped. "Let's focus on our house for now." She poked him gently in the ribs. "Hey, John. Get your head in the game. We lost a worthy competitor, so we only have to beat three teams, not four. We can do this. But only if you focus on what we have to do."

The thought of the unfinished house haunted him as did the image of the family who wouldn't be calling it home. Nevertheless, he directed the movers to the room each piece belonged. After he'd unloaded his car, both he and Cassie drove back to his apartment and packed their vehicles with more items—some salvaged, some not—to decorate the various rooms. Back at the reno house, they emptied boxes and put linens and dishes away.

He pointed to the rug that he and Cassie had laid on the wooden floor in the living room. "No, it goes the other way."

She looked down at the rug and the dimensions of the room. "Are you sure? This seems right."

"It is." He placed two fingers in the space between his eyebrows and pinched the skin slightly. "I'm sorry, Cassie."

"You have a headache? I've got aspirin."

It was more than a headache. It was the knowledge that he knew he was about to suggest something so ludicrous that Cassie would likely fire him from the team. "We need to decorate the house next door, too."

Just as he suspected, her mouth dropped open and she stared at him. "Are you kidding? We haven't completed this house. The one we're going to be judged on. And you want us to waste time on the house next door?"

"It wouldn't be wasted, Cassie—"

"No."

"Just listen to me."

She marched into the kitchen, where boxes littered the floor. He followed her and put a hand on her back. "Cassie, it's the right thing to do. That family shouldn't be punished because they got stuck with a team who wanted to win no matter the cost. They shouldn't have to pay that price."

"I love that in your heart you feel it's the right thing to do. That you're so compassionate of others. But now is just not a convenient time for this."

"I've bought more things than we can use here. I can ask the other designers for their castoffs. Maybe ask neighbors on the street for donations."

"When? I need you here staging the

house." She glanced at her watch. "We have a little more than twenty-four hours and that's it."

He knew she was right. They had judges reviewing the homes the next morning, and time was tight. But he couldn't let it go. "I have to do this."

"This is not one of the twists courtesy of the Belvedere Foundation."

"It's not all about winning, Cassie."

She stared at him for a moment. Then she clenched her jaw, and he could see the war going on in her eyes. "It is for me."

CASSIE SET THE table under the stained glass light and stood back before moving the shade an inch to the right. There. Perfect.

She glanced around the kitchen at the boxes left to unpack. John had decided to set up the bedrooms and media center by himself. Part of it she knew was because of his disappointment in her attitude. She felt badly, but they had too much going on for him to be working at a house that didn't belong to them. He owed himself and the team his total focus. They'd come too far to lose sight of the finish line.

She opened the next box and pulled out a clay bowl painted in colors that mirrored those in the stained glass dome. She placed the bowl on the island and pictured bananas in it that would be handed to the Tanner boys for a snack or sliced to go on top of their cereal. The dishes he'd bought picked up the gray flecks in the countertop. The glasses had a hint of the same blue that matched the cushions on the window seat and other kitchen chairs. It all fitted together.

She had thought they did, too. That they complemented each other. But she couldn't get behind his notion of working on the other house, as well.

A soft knock on the front door. Cassie shook the thoughts away and left the kitchen to answer the door, but John beat her there. It was the Tanner family. Jo gave them a pained smile. "I know we're not supposed to be here until tomorrow morning, but I brought something for John."

Cassie and John stepped back to let them inside. Donny firmly held the hands of the squirming boys while Jo held out a stack

of picture frames. "You had asked for family pictures."

He nodded and took them from her. "Thank you."

There was a moment of awkward silence while the Tanners glanced around the living room. Cassie said, "Since you're here, do you want to see what we've been doing?"

They both nodded, and Jo reached for the hands of both boys while Cassie led them down the hallway to the bedrooms. "We're not quite finished here."

"That's okay," Donny answered. "We'll see it all done soon enough." He entered the master bedroom and whistled. "This looks completely different."

Cassie appreciated his enthusiasm, although she noted the mattress that was propped against one wall, the plush rug that was still rolled up and a box of linens. The old door that John had repurposed for their headboard was the only thing in place. "That's really kind of you."

Jo approached the intricate customized closet, letting go of her sons' hands. Her jaw had dropped. "This is amazing. Did you actually make this?"

Cassie gave a shrug, as if it didn't matter. But she was pleased that Jo recognized her workmanship. "It's nothing big. Just some shelves."

Jo laughed. "No way. This is huge. I've never had such a beautiful closet. I'll be able to get so much stuff in here."

Cassie led them out of the master bedroom, but John sprinted past her to close the doors to the boys' bedrooms. "If you don't mind, I'd like to keep these a surprise until the reveal." He suggested they try the media room, where he'd designed built-in bookcases with extra storage space. A large, comfy sectional sofa and two beanbag chairs faced the massive flat-screen television she'd hung on the wall the day before. John had found a small popcorn machine and neon lights that looked like a concession stand to include in the room. "But this…"

The boys ran into the room, heading straight for the beanbags. They sank into them and clapped their hands. "Movie, movie!" they cried.

Donny smiled and took a seat on the couch before pulling Jo down on his lap. "This is perfect. Better than I had imagined."

John pointed to the sectional. "I chose this since you could fold it out to use for guests if you need to. And the fabric is treated to keep it free from stains and sticky fingers. Wipes off with a wet cloth."

Jo covered her face and started to weep. Cassie sat down next to her. "What's wrong?"

"It's too much. We had hoped and dreamed, but it's more than I expected."

"And you haven't seen it all."

Jo shook her head. "I don't think I can take any more tonight. We'll save the rest. Come on, Donny. Boys, take my hand. We should go."

Donny stood, reluctantly it seemed, since he had perhaps hoped to see more. "The boss has spoken."

The Tanners made for the living room and Cassie and John followed them. The couple seemed to be trying to soak it all in, even though Cassie knew the team was still hours away from finishing. Furniture still needed to be moved into place. Decorations put out. Pictures hung. Donny put one arm around one of his sons and the other arm around Jo. "Thank you for doing this for us." He glanced next door at the dark, lonely-looking house. "Any word what will happen with the Murphys' place?"

Cassie frowned. "The Murphys?"

Jo nodded. "The family that would have moved in beside us. Nice couple with a little girl. The wife is going through cancer treatment, and the medical bills eat up what savings they might have set aside for a house. They were really looking forward to moving in."

John looked at Cassie, and she knew what he was thinking. That they needed to finish up the work on that house. That there were things more important than winning. She rubbed at her temples. "The Belvedere Foundation hasn't yet shared what's going to happen."

"It's a shame." Donny hiked one of the boys onto his hip. "We should leave so you can finish things here." He tried to smile, but his eyes watered. "We really appreciate what you've done for us. Thank you."

Jo stepped forward and engulfed Cassie

into a tight hug. "Thank you for everything."

Cassie and John stood on the bare covered porch that still needed to be decorated to watch the Tanners get their boys into the car and drive away. She waved as they drove off, then turned to John. "We finish this house first, then we go next door. Agreed?"

He smiled and stepped forward to kiss her quickly. "Agreed."

He walked into the house whistling, and she touched her lips. Then she pulled out her phone and called the Buttuccis. "I've got another job for us to do after the judging. Are you in?"

LATER THAT NIGHT, John reviewed the house, checking each detail. He turned off the lights as he visited every room. He found Cassie sitting on the sofa, looking out the front window. He took a seat next to her. "What are you thinking?"

She turned to him, and the sadness on her face surprised him. He'd expected her to be happy that they'd completed in time. True, it was well after midnight but they

had finished what they had set out to do. All that was left was to present the house to the judges for their review and hand the keys to the Tanner family. She should be ecstatic. He reached out and cupped her cheek. "What's wrong?"

She sniffed and shook her head. "Nothing. The house is beautiful."

"So why the tears?"

"I'm not crying."

"You look like you need to."

He sat back on the couch and waited for her to answer. "I'm fine," she repeated, staring out the window again.

It was a lie. Maybe one that she wanted to believe. But working on this house had changed her. It had certainly changed him. He had entered the contest as a means of exploring a different career opportunity. To go down a different path than the one he'd been on for so long. To see if there was something else out there for him professionally.

But working on the house had opened up more than just his career path. Designing the house with her had shown him the possibilities with her, as well. He could see

a future with her. And as more than someone he could renovate houses with. He saw a chance for love, too.

The question was, did she?

She glanced at him. "I've never had a project that I put everything into before. And now it's over. I guess I'm sad that it is."

He reached over and took her hand in his. "It doesn't have to be over."

She nodded. "I know. We're going to finish the house next door, but after that…" She shook her head. "Starting my own company depends on the outcome of this contest."

It sounded like the perfect opening for him. "What do you see in your future?" Who did she see, he wanted to ask, but chickened out at the last moment.

"I love taking houses and making them beautiful. I love the smell of sawdust and the tapping of hammers. I love that when I'm done, I've created a place for a family to live and grow in." She leaned her head back on the sofa. "But sometimes I wonder about what kind of place I could build for my own family." She looked around the living room. "I'd like to come home to a place like this someday."

"You have a house that you're working on."

"It's not the same. I don't have the eye you do for design."

"I could give you some suggestions."

"But I'd still come home to an empty house." She pushed off the sofa and stood, wrapping her arms around her waist. "It's late, and we have to meet the judges here at ten tomorrow morning. We should go."

She shut off the lamp beside the sofa, sending the room into darkness. John followed her outside and waited while she locked the door. The porch light made shadows play on her face as she moved to step off the porch. He reached out and touched her hand to stop her from leaving. When she turned to him, he put his hands on either side of her face and lowered his mouth to hers.

He took his time kissing her. Testing. Teasing. Tasting. She matched him kiss for kiss, bringing her hands up around his neck to pull him closer. He complied and dropped his hands to span her waist and fit her body next to his.

Finally, they broke away and he kissed her gently on the forehead. His heart felt full, something he'd never experienced before. "We'd better stop here."

She took several deep breaths and nodded. "Yes. The neighbors got enough of a show."

He kissed the top of her head. "You don't have to be alone, Cassie. There's something between us, and I think that-"

Her ringing phone interrupted whatever else he had been about to say. She stepped away to answer the call, but then suddenly looked at him with shock. "Can you repeat that one more time?" She closed her eyes and nodded. "Thank you. I'll be right there."

When she hung up, however, she stood there as if frozen in place, clutching her phone. "My father just turned himself in."

CHAPTER TWELVE

CASSIE SAT IN the passenger seat of John's car as he drove them to the police station where they'd detained her father. Despite her gratitude that he'd offered to drive her there, she couldn't face him. She'd hoped that this day would come. That her father would face the charges against him and come back to his family. Now that he had done exactly that, she wasn't sure what she should be doing.

But she did know what she felt. Anger. White-hot fury surged in her veins, growing to a raging fire as they approached the police station. It made her almost blind, unaware of the buildings and streets they passed. She sat silently, unsure if she could voice what she was thinking.

John touched her arm, and she turned to him. "We're here."

She looked out the windshield to see the

police station in front of them. Nodding, she got out of the car and followed him to the lobby, where she gave her name to a sergeant. "Mr. Lowman is currently giving his statement to the detective, but you'll be free to see him once he's finished."

"My mother?"

"She's with him."

Cassie raised an eyebrow at this. She had expected that her mother would show up, but not to sit with him while the detective questioned him. Had she brought a lawyer, too?

The station door opened, and Andromeda ran toward them. The sisters hugged each other tightly. "Thank you for calling me, Andie."

Andie looked over Cassie's shoulder. "Have you seen him yet?"

She shook her head. "Mother's with him and the detective."

"I can't believe he came back." Tears slipped from the corners of Andie's eyes. "I thought we'd lost him forever."

"I know." Cassie led her sister to a chair and sat with her, holding her hand. "But he's doing the right thing."

"The right thing would have been not to steal in the first place."

Cassie winced, then looked to John. He'd been so kind to drive her there, but she didn't want him watching her and her family fall apart. "You don't have to stay. I can get a ride home from my family."

He nodded, his expression soft, caring. "If you need anything, call me."

She gave a weak smile and turned her attention back to Andie, who pawed through her purse before pulling out a tissue to dab her eyes. She put an arm around Andie. "We're going to be okay. So is Daddy."

She watched as John walked to the exit and paused before leaving the station. She had wanted to call him back, to ask him to stay. But it wasn't fair to get him involved in this mess with her family. Now that he was gone, she missed having him there. She dismissed those thoughts because they disturbed her. Brought up more questions than she was willing to explore.

"John was sweet to drive you here."

"We were finishing up at the house when you called."

Andie pulled out another tissue from her

purse and handed it to Cassie. "You might want to wipe the rest of the lipstick from your mouth. Looks like it got smeared by kissing."

Cassie colored but accepted the tissue. "We're just friends."

"Based on the color on his lips, I'd say that you passed that line a while ago. And don't tell me you always wear lipstick. I've been trying to get you to put on makeup for years."

"We're not here to talk about me and John. We're here for Daddy."

Andie gave a shrug. "Feels safer to talk about your relationship with John instead."

Safe wasn't a word that Cassie would have used to describe their relationship. She mentally replaced that word with friendship. They were friends. Partners. Coworkers, really. So why was she still thinking about the way he'd kissed her? It hadn't felt safe in his arms earlier. It had felt scary. But an exhilarating scary. As if she was standing on the edge of something important. Something life changing. All she had to do was trust in herself and in John. But that would be a risk, a dangerous one. It was much easier to stay right where she was. That was safe. That was smart.

A door opened and their mother walked out, followed by Detective August. Cassie glanced behind them to see her father sitting at a table, his head in his hands, gaze fixed on the flat surface in front of him. The door closed behind them, and she shifted her eyes to her mother. She held her arms out to both her and Andromeda.

The three of them hugged for a long moment. "How is he?" Cassie eventually asked.

"Tired. Sad. Perhaps a little defeated."

"Can we see him?" Andie's voice shook with emotion. "For just a minute?"

Their mother looked at Detective August, who gave a short nod. "But one at a time and only for a minute or two," he told them. "We'll be transporting him to a holding cell shortly."

Cassie motioned to Andie. "You should see him first. You're the oldest."

Andie gave a weak smile and put a hand on Cassie's shoulder. "Thank you."

After her sister followed the detective

into the interrogation room, Cassie turned to her mother. "How are you doing?"

Her mother ran her fingers through her hair, giving it a fluff. "It's two in the morning and I'm standing in the middle of a police station wondering what is about to happen to my husband, your father."

"You didn't answer my question."

Her mother's chin quivered, then stilled. "I'll be fine." Her back seemed to straighten, making her taller. "I'm stronger than this situation."

Cassie nodded. "You always have been." Her mother's eyebrows lifted in what might have been surprise. Cassie put her arms around her mother and squeezed. "I didn't see it before, but you've kept this family together. We look to you for strength. Encouragement. And we don't thank you nearly enough for it."

"Cassandra, I don't know what to say."

"Then don't say anything. I love you, Mother."

The hug tightened as her mother pulled her closer. When the interrogation room door opened, the spell was broken and they stepped apart. Andie exited, holding a tissue to the corner of one eye. She gave a nod to Cassie.

Detective August opened the door for Cassie, and she took a seat across from her father. He looked even older than when she'd seen him a few weeks before. Sympathy replaced the anger she'd been feeling earlier. "Daddy."

"Well, you got what you wanted." He brought up his head and placed his cuffed hands in front of him on the table. "Isn't this what you wanted to see? Turning myself in and off to jail?"

"What I wanted was for you to be the hero I had in my mind."

"Now you know I never was."

"You could still be."

He shook his head and put his hands back in his lap, the handcuffs clicking against each other. "What's done is done. Nothing I can do to change it now."

"What did the detective say will happen?"

"I go before the judge and face up to the charges." He dropped his gaze back to the table. "I'm looking at ten to twenty years in prison. This is probably the closest you'll get to me for the next decade." He shook his head. "I'm no hero. Never was. You need to let go of that, baby girl."

A knock on the door, and they both turned to look at Detective August, who stood in the doorframe. "Let's go, Miss Lowman."

Cassie stood and stared down at the part in her father's hair. The gray turning to white near the roots. She wasn't sure if she should hug him. Kiss him on the cheek and tell him she loved him. Because he was right. They wouldn't be this close again for a long time. Making up her mind, she walked around the table and put her arms around her father's shoulders. "I love you, Daddy. Don't give up on being my hero."

She placed a swift kiss on the top of his head before leaving the room, not daring to look back. She didn't want to remember her father that defeated. She wanted to cling to the image of the two of them working side by side as they framed a new window. Or painted a room, singing along to the radio and laughing when one of them sang the wrong words. She wanted to cherish her earliest memory of her daddy lifting her high in the sky as she spread her arms out to fly.

Could he ever be that same man again?

JOHN HAD HOPED to arrive at the house before Cassie the next morning, but the sight of her truck parked at the curb dispelled that idea. He parked behind her and grabbed the note cards he'd written last night when he couldn't sleep. He had one for each room, pointing out the unique features of the design. He hoped the place would impress the judges.

He exited his car and strode up the sidewalk to the house, noting with satisfaction that the flowers Mrs. Lowman had planted had bloomed and accented the edge of the new covered porch. Things couldn't look better.

If only Cassie did. Dark circles under her eyes and the hollows in her cheek told him that she had not slept much the night before. She had dressed up for the occasion in a short-sleeve blouse and skirt in a soft peach color, with strappy sandals. He whistled at her. "You clean up good."

She tried to smile but failed. "I borrowed

this outfit from my sister." She eyed him curiously. "You don't look so bad yourself."

"What? This old thing?" He put a hand to his tie and straightened it. "A good luck gift from my mother."

"We don't need luck. We did our best. Now it's up to the judges."

Cassie took a sip of her coffee while John wondered if he should address the elephant in the room. After all, news of her father turning himself in had been broadcast on every radio and television station that morning. Even the newspaper he'd read with breakfast had pictures of him before the scandal had hit. "Cassie—"

She shook her head. "Don't."

"I was just going to say—"

"Please, John. I need to keep my focus here."

He gave a short nod. "Okay. Later then."

The Tanners arrived next without the twins. Jo gave each of them a hug while Donny kept things to a handshake. Jo rubbed her hands together. "I can't wait to see everything."

Donny put his arm around her shoulders. "Patience, Jo."

"You know that's not my strong suit."

A knock on the front door, and everyone turned to see Mr. Belvedere, who was wearing a navy suit with a long-sleeve buttoned-up shirt and bow tie, this time red with navy polka dots. He adjusted his spectacles and greeted each of them by name. "We're just waiting for our other two judges."

He glanced around the living room and walked to the wall of pictures John had hung the day before. Amid the family pictures that Jo had brought, John had also put those of the house from the time the Czarnecks had lived there. The display told the story of the past and looked toward the future.

Once the other two judges arrived, John felt the knot in his stomach tighten. This was it. This was their chance to prove that they could outbuild and outdesign the other teams. He waited while Mr. Belvedere handed clipboards to the judges. "You have the honor of being the first house we're judging today."

John didn't know if that was a good sign or not. Maybe if they were the standard to what every subsequent house was held to, it could work in their favor. Then again, a wow factor in another house could bump them from first place.

Mr. Belvedere turned to John. "Why don't you tell us what was the idea behind your design, John?"

He cleared his throat and flipped through his note cards. He knew he had written something down somewhere about that. Not finding it, he decided to speak from his heart. "The houses we were given all have histories of families that lived there before. And with the Tanners moving in, the house will meld those memories with new ones. It was our hope that we could incorporate that into the design of the home." He motioned to the picture wall. "Which is why we mixed pictures of past and present here.

"And with the introduction of technology into the design, we wanted to add more of the mixture of past and present. New technology fused with good old ideas." He paused. "Sensy, turn the temperature down two degrees."

The HVAC system turned on, blowing

cool air into the room. The Tanners looked at each other and smiled.

"Sensy, play the CD at a volume of three."

Music started to play softly, a jazzy tune full of sax and horns.

The sweet sounds followed them as they went on to the kitchen. Jo gasped and rushed to the brand-new stainless steel double-door refrigerator. She opened the doors and turned to Donny. "This fridge is almost as big as our entire kitchen at the apartment."

Everyone chuckled at her observation. John stepped forward and showed her the monitor on one of the doors. "Sensy, add eggs, milk and bread to the grocery list."

The monitor listed what he had just said, making Jo look at him with big eyes. "That's amazing."

"And easier for you to keep track of what you need for your family."

One of the judges raised his hand. "Can you tell us about the light fixture above the kitchen table? I don't think I've seen anything quite like it."

Cassie stepped forward. "We found it at

a salvage place. It had been discarded by someone who didn't see the worth I could under the dust."

"Exquisite." He marked something on his clipboard, and John shot her a smile that she returned.

They took turns pointing out the different innovations they'd put into the kitchen and then led the group to the mudroom. From the door, they could see the backyard. At first Donny seemed interested in the green features of the washer and dryer, but his gaze slowly shifted to what was outside. John trailed him and opened the garage door. "We figured you'd like to put your tools in here."

Donny nodded and put a hand on the varnished carpenter's bench. "It's almost a full-on man cave, thank you."

The judges joined them and John led them to the garden, where the tomatoes he'd planted months before looked ready to eat. "Jo, we prepared the ground for a full vegetable garden that I'd be happy to help you plant next spring." He walked to the playhouse and placed a hand on the roof. "And this is for the boys. It's got everything they might want for outdoor play." He pulled out the small table he'd refurbished. "I used the old tiles from the bathroom to create the mosaic."

Jo shook her head and placed a hand to her mouth. "It's beautiful."

"And the backyard is now fully fenced, so you can get that dog they want."

They returned to the house, started in the media room, then went across the hall to the twins' bedrooms. John had designed each as a mechanic's garage. He had also built a wooden track at their waist level on one wall with a tunnel that connected to the other twin's bedroom. The dresser looked like a tool chest in red and silver. Car designs drawn by John hung on two walls. "You said they liked cars."

"They love them."

Each boy also had a wall that contained a huge tablet and whiteboard in order to do homework and play games.

Donny looked awestruck. "Unbelievable."

The judges seemed to agree and made notes on their clipboards. Cassie ushered them out of the room and down the hall to the master bedroom. "John's vision for this room was to make everything soft and plush. Whether it was the silver mist color on the walls or the dozens of pillows on the bed and down comforter, he chose things that would bring a sense of comfort and peace." She walked to the headboard and put a hand along it. "He repurposed an old door and painted it navy for contrast with the bed."

"Was it a door from this house?"

Cassie nodded. "It started its life as the front door actually. It's a solid piece of oak that will last for years to come. I have to admit that I was skeptical at first, but as you can see it adds to the ambience of the room. And mirrors the mix of old with new.

"When we gutted the room, we were able to also create a half bath here." She slid the frosted glass door along the wall to reveal it. "You don't have to worry about morning traffic jams in the main bath anymore."

Jo walked inside and shook her head. "Donny can share the one down the hall with the boys. This is now my retreat."

The judges chuckled and made notes.

"We also repurposed some of the tiles discarded from other houses to create the mosaic floor in here."

The last stop was the main bath. "We brought technology in here as well. Sensy, turn on the shower to seventy-two degrees."

Warm water started to spout from the faucet as John pulled the shower curtain back to show them. "We used glass tiles in the shower and mirrored the jade-green-and-ecru design in the floor tiles and bath accessories."

Mr. Belvedere put his hand under the water and gave a nod. "I'd say that is seventy-two degrees. Sensy, turn off the shower."

They ended the tour on the covered front porch, where John had placed a porch swing with bright blue chambray pillows. Jo and Donny took a seat there and let it slowly rock. "We created the covered porch so that the Tanners can sit out here on evenings and watch the neighborhood. I created the mosaic tile table here, as well using tiles from the old kitchen's backsplash."

"I think we've seen everything we need

to. I'll confer with my fellow judges for a moment," Mr. Belvedere said.

He huddled together with the two as John leaned against the porch railing and Cassie joined the Tanners on the swing. She looked up at him and raised her eyebrows. What now? He smiled and watched the judges talking to each other softly.

Finally, Mr. Belvedere stepped forward. "We do have one final question for the Tanners. How did John capture your needs in his design?"

Jo and Donny glanced at each other, then she sat a little forward. "I wanted a safe environment for my children but also one where they could grow and learn." She turned to John. "That bedroom you created for them… I have no words."

"And they gave us our TV room plus a man cave in the garage." Donny grinned. "I can see the boys and me rebuilding an old car in the driveway when they get older."

"The kitchen was more than I had hoped for, as well. So big and bright. The perfect space for us to gather as a family at the end of the day, to reconnect and share our adventures at the kitchen table with the window seat."

Mr. Belvedere scribbled these comments down and gave a nod. "Thank you. And in what way did they miss the mark with what you wanted?"

Another glance at each other. Jo shrugged. "Maybe a shower in the half bath, though with the limited floor space I don't see how that could have happened."

"We tried, Jo, but it would have shrunk your bedroom," Cassie said.

"Mr. Tanner, your thoughts?"

He shook his head. "I got everything I wanted. And more."

The judges nodded and wrote this down as well. Mr. Belvedere thanked everyone for their time. "A photographer will be out to take pictures."

John spoke up. "Mr. Belvedere, about the house next door—"

He frowned. "Yes, it was unfortunate that we had to lose the fifth team."

Donny stood and walked toward him. "John, Cassie and my wife and I have been talking about going in and finishing the work there. I may not know much about carpentry or design, but I can follow directions."

"The other contestants have also volunteered their time. We want to see out the project. On our own time, of course," Cassie added.

Mr. Belvedere looked between them, shaking his head. "I was going to hire a firm to complete the work, but I have to admit it was all going to take some time to arrange. This would be much faster."

"We can make it work." John stood shoulder to shoulder with Cassie. "Please, sir. We'd like the chance. Not for us, but for the family that had planned on moving in."

Finally, Mr. Belvedere nodded. "All right. I can send you the list of what the building inspector said needed to be finished."

Mr. Belvedere smiled. " I look forward to seeing you all when the results are announced. We will be hosting a party at the Whittier the Saturday before Labor Day, so be sure you're there."

The judges left and walked across the street to the next house. John looked over at Cassie. "I say we go home and change clothes and see what work still needs to be done next door."

CASSIE RESTED HER forehead on the upper kitchen cabinet and closed her eyes. Because Nick and his team had been close to the end of the contest, much of the work on their house had already been completed. It needed a tweak here and there. And the building inspector had left a list of six items that had to be fixed before a notice of occupancy would be granted.

The biggest item on the list was that one of these kitchen cabinets blocked the vent for the stove, which meant the cabinets needed to be moved down by two inches. John groaned under the weight of the cabinet. "Are you going to sleep or are you going to make sure this is level and drill it into place?"

She snapped to attention, apologized and checked the level. "A little higher on the left. Wait. Right there." She drilled the screw through the back of the cabinet and into the wall. "I don't understand why Nick didn't realize that he blocked the vent."

John dropped his arms. "I don't think

he was worried about doing things right, since he was sabotaging everybody else."

"And that's the thing. He also sabotaged his own house, too. Granted, it kept the suspicion off him but he still destroyed some of his own effort." She shook her head. "I don't get it."

"He was also the first one to accuse you. That put him on my bad side from the beginning."

Cassie unscrewed the next cabinet while John braced it from below. They had two more to move and reattach. "At least we'll know things are being done right this time."

"Knock knock," came a call from the living room.

"We're in the kitchen," John called.

An older woman entered the kitchen. "Hello. John, you mentioned you needed help finishing this house, so I talked to a few of my neighbors." Half a dozen more people entered the room behind her. "So tell me. What do you need us to do?"

Cassie looked at John, who grinned. "Miss Loretta, thank you. I didn't expect you to volunteer."

Cassie finished screwing the cabinet into

place, then descended the ladder. "Well, what kind of skills do you bring with you?"

One man held up his hand. "I've done my own home repairs, so I know my way around a workbench."

"I can paint and move furniture," said another neighbor.

John grimaced. "We don't have much furniture to move, unfortunately. And there's no money to go buy more."

Loretta put a hand on his shoulder. "You leave that to me, son. We take care of our neighbors around here."

Donny and Jo entered the house as the rest of the neighbors started organizing what needed to be done, introducing themselves and adding to the general din of conversation. Cassie climbed on the ladder and gave an ear-splitting whistle. "Folks, John and I appreciate everything you want to do. We have less than a week to get this place ready for the Murphys. I need those with home repair experience to meet with me here. Those with design or home decorating skills will talk with John. I think if we work together, we can make this a home to be proud of."

Tiny arrived, too, a dozen boxes of Lucille's pizza held above his head. "And I've brought lunch. No one can do anything on an empty stomach."

He placed the boxes on a counter, opened the top one to remove a slice of pizza and stuffed it into his mouth before heading in Cassie's direction. She came off the ladder and put a hand on his shoulder. "Thank you for the food. I didn't think of it."

Tiny shrugged. "Sal offered me a deal."

"I'm going to have you finish the plumbing in the bathroom." She checked behind him. "Where's Biggie?"

"You know how he gets with crowds."

"This isn't much of one, but I'll take all the help I can get. If he wants to check the plumbing connections in the laundry room that should get him away from the main action." She handed the list from the inspector to Tiny. "We should be able to get the rest of this done in the next couple of days. John is going to spearhead the design group, and hopefully we can get this done before the weekend."

"We've been going nonstop for months. What are a few more days?"

She kissed his cheek. "Thank you, Tiny."

She started to ascend the ladder, but he reached up and touched her arm. She looked down at him. "Did you see your dad?"

She gave a nod. The judging that morning and now going full tilt on the Murphy house had delayed her from worrying about her father. Her mother had said she'd text with any updates once her father faced the judge. But there had been no word yet. "He looks so old."

"Maybe because you're seeing him as he really is and not this puffed-up image you've been carrying around in your head."

She bit her lip, considering this. "Maybe."

"Everything will be okay, Cass." He winked and grabbed another slice of pizza before leaving the kitchen.

The group around Cassie waited for orders. She sent one neighbor to give Tiny a hand in the bathroom and recruited another to help her finish moving the cabinets. "All right, folks. Let's make this happen."

BY THE TIME the sun dipped low in the sky, they'd made a good dent in the required repairs, and John had a list of items they'd need to find. He joined Cassie on the back porch, taking a seat on the top step next to her. She rested her head on one fist, her elbows tucked tight to her sides. "You look tired."

She opened one eye and peered at him. "I am tired. It's been a long couple of days."

"That Miss Loretta is something, isn't she? Organizing the neighbors to come and finish this place?" When he'd mentioned that they were taking on the other house, he hadn't expected her to not only pitch in what she could do but to recruit others, as well. "I like this neighborhood. They look out for each other."

"Something tells me that Miss Loretta is a big reason behind that."

"She told me stories about what it used to be like, and I think it sparked something in her to bring that back." He smiled and leaned back on the porch railing. "She found a sofa that we can use. And I have a bunch of items that I didn't use in the Tanner house that I can bring here. Same goes for the other designers. Plus Mr. Belvedere dropped off a check we can use to finish the house."

"I feel bad that the Murphys seem to be getting shortchanged on this." She shook her head. "I don't understand what happened to Nick's budget that all the money is gone before they finished."

"Maybe he wasn't only sabotaging everyone else—"

"And assaulting you."

"He might have been skimming money for his own personal gain."

Cassie winced. "There seems to be a lot of that lately, doesn't there?"

He put a hand on her shoulder. "I didn't mean your father."

"But he was doing that all the same. He's admitted as much." She glanced at her watch. "The judge denied him bond since he's a flight risk, so he'll be sitting in jail until the trial. The detective says he's looking at five years in prison at least. Plus paying back what he stole. Mother will have to sell the house."

"And move in with you?" He raised an eyebrow at this.

She laughed. "I guess my Aunt Sylvia

has said she can stay with her for as long as she needs to. And Andromeda offered her apartment, too."

"Your mom will land on her feet."

"I know she will." She stretched her arms out, groaning at the effort. "We should call it a day. Volunteers are coming over at eight tomorrow morning."

"I'll be here."

He offered her his hand and pulled her to her feet, bringing her close to him. She looked up into his eyes, then her gaze dropped to his mouth. The temptation to kiss her made him forget where they were standing for just a moment. He lowered his mouth to hers, and she melted into his embrace, their hands entwined and resting on his chest.

Then she stepped back, breaking the contact. He swallowed and let go of her hand. "We should go."

She nodded. "We must be tired. That's why I kissed you."

"You mean I kissed you."

She peered at him. "It was mutual."

"Cassie, since the project is over, what happens to us?" The thought had been simmering in the back of his mind. Now that they weren't seeing each other every day at the house, what next? Were they friends? Something more? They'd never talked about it, and he wanted some clarity.

"Us?" She gave a shrug. "Is there an us?"

"That's what I'm asking."

Her phone buzzed, and she pulled it from her pocket, checking the screen. "It's Andromeda. I need to take this."

"We need to talk."

"Later," she said, offering him a smile, and walked away to answer her call.

The thing was, he didn't know if there would be a later for them. Sure, he'd be with her at the farewell gala when the winners would be announced and they'd celebrate the end of the contest. But what then? Did they find a way to work together? They'd made a good team on this project, and he had no doubt that they could translate their success from the contest into future projects.

But that wasn't the question that kept him awake at night. Did Cassie feel the same way he did? That their partnership had evolved into something more? More than friendship?

He watched her walk to her truck and get inside. That talk couldn't wait forever.

CASSIE FELT RELIEF as she hung up the phone. Andie had said that Daddy was being held at the county jail until his trial, but he seemed to be okay. However, the relief wasn't from Andie's call but from escaping the awkward conversation with John.

Part of her wanted to explore the possibility of them being an us, while the other, more rational, side reminded her that she wasn't in any position to pursue a relationship. Her life was a mess and required more attention than she'd been giving it. The contest had served to distract her from the reality of being unemployed. Her father's business had been sold off piece by piece until nothing was left for her to build on. Not even the Lowman name would be left to her without bringing her father's baggage with it.

She shouldn't be thinking about kissing John or wondering how he felt about her.

She had to keep her head focused on the next steps in her career, whatever was left of it after the contest.

Yes, that was what she'd do. She would figure out where she was going in her career and put the question of a relationship with John on a back burner to explore later.

But how much later? She was getting tired of being lonely after putting in long hours at work. She'd like to come home to someone more than her dog. To have someone to eat dinner with. To curl up on the sofa and watch TV with. Someone who would kiss her like John did.

She leaned against her truck and glanced at the Murphys' house. He was right there, and he seemed to like her. Could she have a future with him? Did she want one?

No, any future that she had with John or anyone would have to wait until the question of her career was settled. How could she go to John with nothing?

She got in her truck and put the key in the ignition and drove away.

CHAPTER THIRTEEN

IT WOULD END in the same ballroom that they had started the contest in. Cassie looked down at her dress, the same one she'd worn then, as well. She didn't have the desire to purchase a new outfit that she wouldn't wear again. Even though Andromeda had insisted she needed to wear something else. "What if they compare the pictures from the first party? They'll know you're wearing the same dress," she'd said. But Cassie figured that her money would be better spent on necessities like food and shelter if they didn't win the grand prize.

And they had to win.

Her mother joined her, looking elegant in a silk dress in the same color of blue as her eyes. Though she hadn't approved of Cassie entering the contest, she seemed to have come around, if her presence at the finale was any indication.

Cassie nodded toward the bar. "Can I get you a drink? Wine, maybe?"

"White wine, please." Her mother glanced around the ballroom and narrowed her eyes at someone across the room. "Is that Bill Swenson?"

Cassie followed her mother's gaze. "He wasn't happy that he didn't get picked or that I was chosen."

"When your father left us, that man called me and volunteered to help me out." She shuddered and tugged the lapels of her silk jacket closer together. "I won't give you the details of how he intended to help, but it wasn't decent for young ears."

Cassie glanced back at Bill, frowning. "He hit on you? But you're…"

"I'm not quite dead, Cassandra. Some men tell me that I'm still attractive."

"I was going to say you're still married to Daddy."

Her mother's eyes glistened at the mention, but the look was brief and returned to its usual cool composure. "Right. Your father. Think I'll go powder my nose."

"Mother, I didn't mean to…"

But her mother had already left. Cassie

walked to the bar and ordered a beer for herself and a glass of white wine for her mother. She'd told John that she'd meet him here at the event. The same with the Buttucci brothers. But none of them had yet arrived.

Taking the tall stein and wine glass, she found an empty table that lined the dance floor. That was one thing she hadn't expected when the invitation for this gala had arrived. They were serving dinner and dancing before the winners were announced. She would much rather just get to the results that would determine her future.

"There you are." John stood in front of her. "But we're not at this table."

She frowned and looked at the empty seats. "There's no one here."

"We've been assigned table number seven. Didn't you check in with the hostess when you got here?"

"My mother was busy getting reacquainted with a group of people, so we walked inside."

She stood and followed him to the correct table, where an older woman sat. She reminded Cassie of her own mother, the regal way she held herself, the elegant dress and coiffed hair. John motioned to the woman. "Cassie, this is my mother, Beatrice Robison."

Cassie shot her hand out. "Mrs. Robison, a pleasure."

The woman returned her handshake. "Johnny has told me so much about you. And the house, of course."

"I hope he took you over to see the final product."

"He did. Thank you."

John pulled a chair out for Cassie and waited until she sat before pushing it closer to the table. He turned to his mother. "Can I get you something to drink?"

Beatrice eyed Cassie's beer. "That looks pretty good to me."

That surprised Cassie. She figured that she would have been more of a martini drinker. Or would have preferred a glass of wine, like her mother usually did.

Beatrice asked Cassie, "Did you invite anyone to join you?"

"My mother had to step out for a moment, but she'll be back." Cassie smoothed down the front of her dress. "I hate these kinds of fancy events. I feel like I'm going to make a mistake or say the wrong thing."

Beatrice eyed her. "Johnny told me that you were more comfortable in T-shirts and jeans than in a dress."

He had? Cassie took a sip of her beer, considering that bit of news. "What else has he told you?"

But John's mother gave her a mysterious smile and didn't elaborate. Tiny and Biggie entered the ballroom, and Cassie motioned them over. She'd never seen the brothers in tuxes before. She gave a whistle as they got closer. "You guys look great."

"If we're going to win and be on that stage, I wanted to make sure we looked respectable." Tiny turned to Beatrice. "And who have we here?"

"This is John's mother, Beatrice."

Tiny started to put his hand out to shake hers when Biggie cut in front of him and took the woman's hand in his. He pressed a kiss to her hand. "Mrs. Robison, I am Luigi Buttucci, but you must call me Lou. You are enchanting."

Beatrice blushed and tried to wave away the compliment, but Cassie could see that she was pleased. Even more so when he took the seat on the other side of her.

Tiny raised eyebrows at this. He held out his hand to Beatrice. "And I'm his brother, Tiny." He leaned closer to Cassie. "I've never heard him say so many words to a woman. This should be interesting."

John brought drinks over to the table and greeted both the brothers. If he was surprised by Biggie seating himself next to his mother, he didn't say a word. But Cassie had a feeling that he was going to keep an eye on the two of them the rest of the evening. Her mother returned from the ladies' room looking more composed than she had before and greeted both brothers before John introduced her to his mother.

Mr. Belvedere walked up to the microphone and called for everyone's attention. "Ladies and gentlemen, allow me to welcome you to the Belvedere Foundation's contest finale. We'll be serving dinner in about ten minutes if you'd like to find your seats."

As promised, the servers started bringing out trays of salads and rolls. Out of breath, Jo and Donny arrived at their table.

It looked like Jo had gone to the salon, since her long dark hair was piled expertly on top of her head. She and Donny gave everyone hugs before taking a seat. "Sorry we're late," Jo said. "The babysitter didn't get there until the last minute. Did we miss anything?"

John made the introductions as he passed the basket of rolls to the couple. Talk around the table centered on the contest, conjecturing who would win. Jo was convinced that Cassie and John would take home the grand prize, while those who had worked on the project tried to hang on to that hope but not state it out loud. Cassie, especially, wasn't sure if they had won. Of course, she hadn't seen the other houses, but she would stand by the work they had done on the Tanner home any day.

With the arrival of the entrées of beef and chicken, conversation changed to smaller groups. John leaned over to Cassie, so close that she could smell the scent of his aftershave. "I wish I was as confident as Jo about our chances. What do you think?"

Cassie shook her head. "I honestly don't know. But everything rides on winning."

"About that, Cassie. I've wanted to talk to you about what happens after this contest."

She still wasn't ready for that conversation. She wanted to focus on eating her dinner and keeping it down before the butterflies in her belly revolted. "Now?"

"Well, you've been avoiding me ever since we finished the house."

She knew she had. And she knew that it had hurt him when she hadn't answered his calls. But she couldn't talk about them working together. Or as anything else. Part of it was doubt since she didn't know what would happen in her life if they didn't win. But most of it was fear, if she wanted to be honest. She was afraid of trying to see a future with John, professional or personal. She had no clue what her future would be after this contest. She had spent so much time concentrating on that outcome that she hadn't thought beyond tonight.

They had to win. They just had to.

"I'm sorry, but this isn't a good time." She wiped the corners of her mouth with the linen napkin before returning it to her lap. "We're at a table with our mothers, the Buttucci brothers, the Tanners. I don't want to talk about us with an audience listening in."

"Fair enough. But we need to have that talk."

"I agree, but later."

JOHN ADMITTED HE was hurt that Cassie had pushed him away. They had worked on the Murphy house, but they hadn't shared more than a dozen words during that time and none since they'd completed the house. He had thought they had become more than coworkers, maybe more than friends even, if their few kisses had meant as much to her as they had to him.

That was the part that stung the most. Maybe they hadn't meant anything to her. She was the first woman who had ever truly captured his heart. That had made him yearn for something more. That Cassie didn't feel the same way left him feeling a little lost.

Hadn't they discovered that they made a good team? That the project became better because they respected each other's ideas? That when they combined, they created something stronger, something special, and more than their parts?

He scooted his plate forward, no longer interested in picking at the prime rib or the half-eaten baked potato. His thoughts made him sound like he had a crush on Cassie. But what he felt ran deeper than that. It was hard to imagine a future without her. Did that mean he loved her? He glanced at her as she laughed at something Donny said. Yes, he loved her. Wanted her. He had to get her alone.

The music changed to something people could dance to, and John noticed that several had gathered in the center of the ballroom to do just that. He put his napkin on the table and stood. Tapped Cassie on the shoulder. "Would you dance with me?"

Cassie's eyes widened at his suggestion. "Dance?"

Tiny chuckled from the other side of the table, but John ignored him. "Yes. Dance." He motioned with his thumb to the dance floor. "You and me."

Cassie slipped her hand into his and he led her onto the dance floor. He put his hands on her small waist. She glanced around her, seeming to be unsure of what to do. He leaned forward. "Put your arms on my shoulders."

She did so. "I don't know how to dance."

They swayed in time to the tune. "You seem to be doing okay."

She might have been a little stiff at first but soon followed his lead. He looked down at her as she turned her head toward their table. Then, shaking her head, she closed her eyes and leaned forward so that her cheek rested against his chest.

He moved them around the floor smoothly and slowly until they were across the room from their table. He didn't want an audience at the moment. "Cass, there's something I want to tell you."

She looked up at him, fear behind her eyes. "Don't, John. Don't say it."

"You don't know what I'm going to say."

"You want us to start a business together. And I don't know if I can after tonight."

He paused. Maybe he should keep it safe. For now. "Yes, I do want us to keep working together. We could have a great business future."

"You don't know that. If we don't win—"

"This is about more than winning." He stopped moving and dropped his hands. "This is about you and me. It's about continuing what we've just started. Win or not tonight, we made a beautiful home together. And I don't want to walk away from that partnership."

"We think it's beautiful, but what if the judges don't?"

"I don't care about the judges. I care about you."

The song had ended, making his words carry across the ballroom. Cassie turned back and saw that everyone at their table was watching them. She shook her head. "Don't do this."

"Do what? Tell you how I feel?"

She started to walk away, but he called to her to stop. "Please, Cass. Talk to me. Now. Before they announce the results. Because they don't matter to me. You do."

When she turned to look at him, the fear in her eyes had been replaced by frustration. "Winning may not matter to you, but it does to me. I have to win. I can't bring back the company without the money or the national attention winning the contest will bring."

"So we'll start smaller. It will be okay, Cass. I promise." He reached out and touched her cheek. "We can do it together."

"No." She hung her head. "I need to do this on my own for once. To prove that I'm just as good as my father."

"You're wrong about that. You're so much better than him."

She refused to be convinced, and John realized in that moment that it wasn't just prize money or recognition at risk for her. Failing at this would mean losing her identity. He grasped her to his chest, longing to take away her fear. "You are more than this contest. You are an incredible woman who I'm falling in love with."

She backed away from him to look into his eyes. Instead of joy at his confession, she looked lost and unsure. He peered into her eyes and said, "Win or lose, I love you."

She blinked several times, a single tear falling on her cheek. He reached out and wiped it away with his thumb. "You don't have to be scared, Cass. It's all going to work out."

"I don't know about this, John. I just don't know."

Any further conversation was lost at the arrival of Mr. Belvedere on the stage.

MR. BELVEDERE WAS at the microphone again, but now the tension in the room had significantly increased. Cassie put a hand to her belly. She shouldn't have eaten that prime rib. Her nerves had tied her stomach in a knot, and she was paying for it now. She closed her eyes and took a few deep breaths. Someone clasped her hand, and she peeked to find that John had returned to her side.

She had regretted the words after she'd said them. Hated how the look in his eyes had dimmed and been replaced by hurt. She wanted to take them back but they had been said, and she couldn't change it. Maybe she was placing too much importance on this win. But she couldn't help how she felt, right? This had been her entire focus for the last few months, and it would all end in a few minutes. No matter the outcome.

Mr. Belvedere smiled and nodded to the

band. "Thank you for the wonderful music provided by Sally Hart and the Hartbeats."

Polite applause. But was everyone thinking "let's get on with this," like she was?

"Before we announce the winners of our first annual Belvedere Take Back the Neighborhood contest, I'd like to read a letter I received yesterday." He pulled a small folded sheet of paper from his breast pocket and put on reading glasses. He scanned the room over the top of the letter, then started reading. "Dear Mr. Belvedere. Words cannot express our joy at your news earlier this week. We want to thank each person who worked tirelessly to complete our home. Our family will be moving in as originally planned because of the selflessness of those who saw a need and stepped in to help. We were told that neighbors stepped in as well as contractors and designers. We look forward to being a part of such a welcoming community. Thank you and bless you. The Murphy family."

He paused and again looked out over the crowd. "They couldn't come tonight, but I'd like to recognize those who gave of their own time. Will those who helped finish the Murphy home please stand and receive this thanks?"

Everyone at their table but the mothers stood, as well as many around the room, while applause filled the ballroom. Cassie glanced around, and the panic she'd been experiencing started to dissipate. John had been right about finishing the house. It wasn't about the contest but about helping a family who couldn't have done it themselves. She turned to him and gave him a smile.

The applause died down as they took their seats again. Mr. Belvedere removed his glasses and put them in his pocket along with the letter. "When we started discussing what the Belvedere Foundation could do to further help our communities, someone had this unique idea of transforming a neighborhood by rehabbing abandoned houses. Well, this bloomed into the reason we're here tonight. Five run-down houses have been transformed into beautiful homes that will belong to five families who dreamed of owning their own home one day but had given up hope. We chose five designers and five contractors that we believed held those same ideals. Eight of you have reached this final point in the contest. The judges and I were astounded by the workmanship and creativity we saw, and I'll admit that deciding the winners was a difficult choice for us. Would the four teams and the families who will soon move into their new homes please come up and join me on the stage?"

Applause as Cassie stood and followed John to the front of the ballroom. When they reached the stage, John held his hand out to her to help her up the stairs. She took it and squeezed it. This was it. This was *it*. They gathered behind Mr. Belvedere near the middle of the stage. Her team clasped each other's hands as Mr. Belvedere pulled out another sheet of paper that listed the teams.

"In fourth place, we have the Sanela and Geller team. Their design incorporated natural elements with a focus on environmental and green products and technologies."

The team stepped forward to accept congratulations from the judges and returned to their seats. John leaned toward Cassie. "One team down. I have a good feeling about this."

Cassie wished she shared his enthusiasm.

Mr. Belvedere announced, "In third place, we have the Potter and Wieczorek team who used heirlooms from their family to create a unique style suited for them."

More applause and congratulations. That left two teams. Cassie raised her eyes to the ceiling. *Please let us win. We have to win this. Please please please.*

Tiny nudged her, and she turned to see him nodding. "This is it, Cassie."

Yes, it was. Everything they had been working toward was about to be over. But hopefully that meant they would be able to turn it into a new opportunity with the prize money. A new chance for them all.

Mr. Belvedere turned to the audience. "I wish we could have two winners because these two teams surpassed our wildest dreams. The judges and I struggled with who should take the top spot and, after much debate and discussion, we decided on one team that had that something extra. They took the parameters of the contest, the needs of their family and expanded it to include the purpose of community."

Cassie's heart almost stopped. "It's us. It's gotta be us, right?"

John looked at her. "I meant what I said before. No matter the outcome, I love you."

She looked back at him, wanting to echo his words. The drummer in the band started a low drumroll, adding to the tension. Cassie's team pulled each other in close for a huddle, prepared to hear the news. Prepared to celebrate because they had to win.

Mr. Belvedere cleared his throat. "The winners of the first annual Belvedere Foundation Take Back the Neighborhood contest are…" He paused, and Cassie wanted to yell at him as she did at the television screen when the host waited for dramatic effect. "The Beckett and Sterling team."

Streamers poured down from the ceiling as the applause and hollers filled the ballroom. Cassie made sure to smile when she approached Beckett with an outstretched hand. "Congratulations."

Beckett shook her hand. "I heard what you guys did for the house next door. It should have been you that won."

A loud bang came from the kitchen. Beckett shuddered. She squeezed his hand.

"It's okay, Beckett. It was probably just a tray that fell."

He straightened, looking both abashed and angry. "Sorry. I don't do well with crowds." He glanced around the crowded ballroom. "I gotta go."

She glanced over at her team, who looked somberly at her. Trying to keep the smile on her face, she failed. "I'm sorry we didn't win."

Jo rushed forward and engulfed her in a hug. "Don't be. We have an amazing home and garden because of the work you and your team did. I'm not sorry."

Cassie put her arms around Jo. "I really wanted to win."

"We all did." Jo stepped back and looked into Cassie's eyes. "But this doesn't make you a loser."

Then why did it feel like she was? She took a deep breath and tried to keep it together. Because inside she knew that she'd just lost everything.

JOHN WATCHED CASSIE, who seemed to be on autopilot as she accepted her congratulations from the judge. He could almost see the defeat she had put on like a shawl around her shoulders. He wanted nothing more than to take it off her, but the only one who could do that was her.

The judge shook his hand heartily. "I really wanted your team to win. The way you repurposed items and modernized them was nothing more than spectacular. I hope you continue your career. You're truly gifted."

John nodded his thanks and pondered the judge's words. He wanted to continue what they had started, but without Cassie that wouldn't happen. She inspired him. Challenged him. Made him and his ideas better. And if she wasn't going to be involved, he didn't know if he could continue.

He turned to Cassie and put a hand on her shoulder, but she shrugged it off. "Don't, John. I don't want to hear how we didn't really lose. Because if we're not the winners, then what does that make us? Right. The losers."

She pushed past the group that had gathered around the winning team and fled the ballroom. John turned to Tiny. "Is she going to be okay?"

Tiny's eyes followed her as she exited the room. He shook his head. "Those words she just said? She heard them from her father enough times that I think she's started to believe them. I hope she can bounce back, but I don't know."

"What about you and Biggie?"

Tiny glanced behind him at his brother, who stood silently watching the crowd. "We always land on our feet. Maybe it's time we look at retirement."

"Are you ready for that?"

He laughed, but the sound dripped with bitterness in John's ears. "Besides Cassie, who's going to hire two old carpenters and painters?"

"I'd hire you."

Tiny gave him a smile and put his hand on John's shoulder. "We'll take you up on that offer if you need us. It was a pleasure working with you."

The two men shook hands and then left the stage. At the foot of the platform, Jo and Donny waited for him. Jo wrapped her arms around him. "I wish we had won."

"That makes two of us."

Donny held out his hand, and John shook it vigorously. "Thank you for all your hard work."

Jo glanced around them. "We wanted to thank Cassie, too, but I lost her in this crowd."

She couldn't be found because she didn't want to be. John gave a short nod. "I'll be sure to let her know when I see her next." If he ever saw her again.

"We're having a barbecue a week from Sunday if you'd like to join us. I want to break in a new grill while we still have nice weather." Donny turned to Tiny and Biggie. "You two are also invited. I'm thinking steaks, and Jo makes a fabulous bacon dip you need to try."

John nodded. "I'll bring dessert and my mom, if that's okay."

"I'll be there," Biggie said, looking at John.

Tiny shook Donny's hand. "We'll bring something, too. I may not cook much, but I know how to pick out a great veggie tray. Do your boys like ranch?"

Jo laughed. "They eat everything, those

two." She turned to John. "Please invite Cassie, as well."

He would try. He would reach out to her, but he couldn't guarantee if she would reach back.

CHAPTER FOURTEEN

THE TANNERS' BACKYARD had filled with neighbors and friends as Donny manned the grill. He held up a hand in greeting as John entered the backyard. "Jo says to take food into the kitchen. Then help yourself to a beer from the cooler and help me with these steaks. That is, if she doesn't find another job for you to do first."

John went inside and found Jo in the kitchen. She was directing several people about where to put food they'd brought to the barbecue. She smiled at him as he placed a cherry pie on the end of the counter, where someone else had placed a whole watermelon. She searched drawers and sighed. "Why Donny's brother couldn't cut the watermelon before bringing it, I don't know."

John glanced down at the whole pie. "I didn't cut the pie yet, but if you've got another knife I can."

She handed him a knife. "Please, and thank you." She turned to someone who asked a question about where to put salads. "They go over there by the window." She started to cut into the watermelon, but she didn't have the strength to make it through the thick rind.

"Here. Let's trade." He handed her his knife and took the larger butcher one from her and plunged the knife into the melon.

"Thanks."

As they sliced the pie and fruit, Jo looked up at him. "Did you hear from Cassie?"

Eight calls, and they had all gone unanswered. He shook his head. "She's off licking her wounds, I think. Don't take it personally." Not that he'd followed his own advice.

"She's got nothing to be ashamed of." Jo looked around the kitchen. "She made this beautiful place for us."

"All she knows is that we lost." And he'd lost her. He motioned to the watermelon. "Do you want this in slices or cubes?"

"Slices. Let me find you a platter to put them on." She rummaged through cupboards and, finally finding what she wanted, handed him a tray. "We've been here almost a week, and I'm still searching for stuff."

"I'm surprised you got everything unpacked in a week."

She shook her head. "We haven't. Just don't look in the media room. I told Donny that if we were having company on Sunday, we had to get the kitchen unpacked and ready. Everything else could wait." She paused, a soft smile on her lips. "Well, the kitchen and the boys' rooms."

Just as she mentioned her sons, one of them zoomed through the kitchen on his way outside. "Milo, slow down." She shook her head. "He's only got one setting. Fast-forward."

She positioned the wedges of watermelon on the platter. "I don't see how we lost. I know the judges decided on the other team, but you and Cassie are winners in my eyes. The way you transformed this house is spectacular. People should see the work you did."

"We'll get some regional recognition. It may not be national television, but it's something."

She smiled and patted his arm. "You didn't bring your mom?"

John grimaced. "Biggie said he would pick her up and bring her himself."

"That's so sweet."

He could think of other words for it, but he had promised his mother that he would be polite. He was happy that his mother had finally moved on from his father. And as for her choices, she could do worse. But still. Biggie Buttucci?

Speaking of Buttuccis, Tiny entered the kitchen and handed off a large vegetable tray with ranch dip to Jo. He nodded to John. "I didn't get a hold of Cassie. Did you?"

"I think she's avoiding us all."

Tiny sighed. "That's what I was afraid of. The contest gave her a sense of purpose." Tiny eyed John. "Can you think of a new project we could bring her in for?"

John shook his head. "I was hoping you'd know of something."

"I'll keep an ear out." He started to leave the room but then turned back to face John. "Someone who loved her wouldn't give up on her."

"I'm not the one who gave up."

"Just saying. If I were in love with her, I wouldn't stop pestering her. I'd camp out on her front porch if I had to."

The idea tempted John.

Tiny went to join the group outside on the patio. Jo handed John a cantaloupe. "Might as well cut this, too." She watched him slice into it then scoop out the seeds. "I had always thought you and Cassie were a couple."

"I'm not even sure if we're friends anymore."

"I saw the way she looked at you when you were dancing the other night. There was more than friendship there."

He mulled that over as he finished cutting the melon into wedges.

Later, in the backyard, he joined Donny, who stood at the grill with another man. When John approached them, the other man acknowledged him. "Donny told me you were here. John, right?"

John nodded. "Yes. And you are?"

"Ian Murphy from next door."

John smiled and nodded. "Of course."

"When Donny said you'd be here today,

I had to meet you." He looked behind him. "Is your girlfriend here?"

"Girlfriend?"

Donny leaned in. "He means Cassie." He shook his head as he used tongs to turn over hot dogs on the grill. "John keeps insisting that they're just friends, but we know what we see. There's something there."

"She's not coming."

"Oh." Ian looked disappointed but gave a shrug. "She doesn't know what she's missing. And I don't mean Donny's burnt hot dogs."

"They're not burned." Donny peered at the meat, wincing. "They're just a little darker than normal."

Ian laughed and slapped Donny on the back, but John had a difficult time putting a fake smile on his face. He started to ease away and turned to find Miss Loretta handing him a bottle of water. "You look thirsty."

He accepted the bottle but didn't open it. "Thanks."

"You're also looking a little lost."

He guessed that he was. With the contest, his days had been filled with working on the house. Now that it was over, he felt a little at loose ends. A friend of his mother's had asked him to come look at her house and give an estimate of what it would cost to update the kitchen. But he didn't know anything about that. That was Cassie's domain. He could recommend ways to paint and decorate, but completely redoing the kitchen wasn't his expertise. "I'm mulling over my career options now that the contest is over."

Loretta peered at him, but shook her head. "No, it's about that woman." She looked around the backyard. "Cassie didn't come today?"

"She hasn't answered any of my calls, and I left her about eight voice mails about today." He gave a shrug. "She doesn't want anything to do with me."

"Have you given her a chance?"

"Eight voice mails, Miss Loretta."

"So call again and leave her a ninth. And a tenth." She put a hand on his arm. "Do you want her to be a part of your life? If so, you don't give up after eight calls. And you don't depend on a phone call to do what you should say in person."

John cracked open the bottle and gulped the water. In person? Trying to talk to her over the phone seemed a safer option. He couldn't be made a fool of that way. "I don't know."

"What don't you know? Do you have doubts over her feelings?" She peered at him. "There comes a time in everyone's life where they have to decide whether they let the doubts rule their lives or if they make a grand gesture to get what they want. Is this the time or not? Only you can say."

The doubts were loud in his head, but if Miss Loretta was right then it was time for the grand gesture. Whether Cassie accepted him or not, at least he'd know for sure.

It had been days since she'd lost what she saw as her future. It sounded a bit melodramatic, but there it was. As she sat waiting for her father in the visiting room of the county jail, she felt as bleak and hopeless as the dull gray walls and hard metal tables and chairs there. She had tried her best, and she had still lost.

Her mother had reminded her that she

would bounce back. That she had an unwritten future ahead of her where she could do anything she wanted. Well, she'd done what she wanted, but she hadn't been good enough.

She guessed that was what all this gloom was about. She'd never be good enough to run her own company. To be her own boss.

To finally earn her father's praise.

The door opened, and her father shuffled in behind two other inmates. She stood as he entered, surprised how old and feeble he'd become in such a short time. He frowned when he saw her and ambled to the table where she sat. "Cass, why are you here?"

"I promised I would come." She took a seat across from him, wanting to reach out and give him a hug or touch his hand, but she'd been warned by the guards that touching wasn't permitted. "How have you been?"

Her father gave a shrug. "Fine, I guess. The food stinks. The cot is hard and uncomfortable. But at least I get my hour outside every day."

Sad to find that her dad's life had been

reduced to what he ate, where he slept and how he enjoyed an hour. She longed to give him some comfort. Maybe he'd adjust in time. She feared what would happen to him if he hung on to this defeated attitude.

And what about your own? She brushed away the thought and held out an envelope, pushing it across the table toward him. "Mother and Andromeda asked me to bring you their letters."

He nodded and pulled the envelope to him. "Nice of you."

"Biggie and Tiny also asked me to tell you they're thinking about you."

"What are those brothers up to now?"

"Since we lost—" She choked on the word. It still hurt to talk about it. "They're talking about retiring."

"Those guys won't retire. They'll find another contractor eventually. They can't help working."

She nodded and dropped her gaze to her hands. "Tom Watterson is buying Mother out. The house. The last of the company's assets. All of it."

Her father was only inches away from her. So close, yet he still seemed so far away. "He'd be a good man to work for. You should approach him about a job."

She raised her head at his words. "I don't want to work for Watterson."

"He could teach you a lot."

"I learned everything I needed to know from you." She scowled at him, rising to her feet despite a nearby guard's warning. She glanced at the guard, then took her seat again, dropping the volume of her voice. "Because of you, I know how to run my own company. How to bid on and negotiate contracts. How to plan a project and keep a team on task."

He held out his hands. "So then why aren't you working for yourself?"

"You know why." She crossed her arms over her chest. "It takes money to start a company. And where am I going to find enough to do that?"

"By starting small and building from there. How do you think I did it?"

She laughed and looked around the visitors' room. He grimaced. "Okay, so I'm not a stellar example of how to run a business. But you know plenty of people who are."

"Because of my last name, no contractor wants to talk to me."

"I meant the Buttuccis. The three of us started Lowman Construction together. Biggie may not say much, but his words of wisdom helped us get off the ground those first few years." He leaned forward. "Have you even talked to them about this?"

"Dad, we lost the contest. We came in second place, but they might as well have plastered big capital Ls on our foreheads."

"So you lost one contest. You move on to the next."

She let her head droop forward. "I can't."

"Why not? Cass, you said it yourself. You know everything you need to know to succeed in this business, so what's really stopping you?"

Her eyes watered, and she couldn't bear to face him. "I don't know."

"Yes, you do, Cass. Tell me."

She shook her head, but he reached out and touched her hand. A guard approached the table and rapped his knuckles on the metal surface. "No touching, Lowman. You know the rules."

Her father nodded and sat back in the metal chair. "What are you afraid of?"

The tears now streamed down her cheeks as she faced him. "What if I can't do this without you? What if I'm not good enough to do it on my own?"

Her father stared at her silently as she batted away her tears. She hated to cry, especially in front of him. Ashamed of the tears, she glanced away.

"You've always been good enough."

She jerked her chin up at those words. He'd never said them to her. He'd always criticized her work, pointing out the faults and making her start over again. Her father sighed. "First off, you wouldn't have made it into the contest if you hadn't been good enough."

"But we didn't win—"

"And are you going to let that define you?" He wearily eyed the room. "I know it's pretty ironic coming from me as I sit in jail, but you can't let that one moment determine the rest of your life. Don't let it be a stop sign. Turn it into motivation to win the next one. To go out there and prove to everyone that you're good and that you believe in yourself." He swallowed hard. "Better than even your old man."

She closed her eyes for a moment. She wanted to believe that losing wasn't the end of her dream. That it was just a small dip in the road, rather than the bottomless canyon it seemed on her trip to success.

Her father continued, "So do you have the courage to try again?"

Could she reach deep down and find the strength to try once more? She might have spent years trying to be more like her dad, but she had pieces of her mother inside her, too. Her mother wouldn't give up after losing. She'd figure out a way to come back even stronger than before. Maybe it was time to accept her father for who he was and to become more like her mother.

She opened her eyes, and he smiled. "That's my girl."

CASSIE PULLED INTO the driveway of her house to find John sitting on her front porch, a rolled newspaper in his hand. He looked good. More than good. The warm weather had lingered into September, and he wore a T-shirt and jeans that highlighted how fit he was. He'd called her several times a day since the contest, but she hadn't answered the phone once. Being with him only reminded her of the loss. She took a deep breath before opening the door and getting out of the truck. He stood as she crossed the lawn to the front porch.

She looked him over. "Hey, there. What are you doing here?"

He held out the newspaper to her. "I thought you might like to see the article on page three."

"I don't."

He lowered his arm, the paper still in his hand. "You haven't been returning my calls. I got tired of waiting for you to pull yourself out of this hole you've put yourself in."

"I didn't put myself there. Losing did."

"You're not going to win everything, Cassie. And the point of all this is what you do when you fall. Do you stay down or do you get back up?"

"John—"

"Please, hear me out." He paused, then dove right in as if taking a leap of faith. "You drive me crazy. But then I guess when you fall in love with someone, the things that make you love them are the same things that get under your skin."

Her heart skipped a beat before resuming. He still loved her even after all this? "I know what you're going to say, Cass. That it's too soon and not right that I'm in love with you. But you'd be wrong about that, too." He sighed. "When I first met you, I didn't realize I was seeing my future. And I don't mean just the construction and design business. But everything." He ran a hand through his hair. "I'm messing this all up."

"I'd say you're on a roll."

He put the newspaper in her hands. "Page three. It says it much better than I ever could."

She unrolled the paper to find it was the local Detroit newspaper's real estate section. She looked up at him. "Page three?"

He nodded and sat on the porch while she turned the pages. Page three showed pictures of the Tanner home as well as an announcement of the grand opening of the CJ Construction and Design Company. In bold letters along the bottom, it read:

Cassie, be my partner in business and in life. Let's design a beautiful life together.

"Wow."

He looked nervous. "Too much?"

She smiled and shook her head.

He stood and put his hands in hers. "Then say yes, Cass. The Tanner house proves that we're better together than apart. I can't make this work without you. I don't want to."

She looked into his eyes. "If, and I mean if, we do this, it doesn't mean I'm always going to agree with you. Or that I'll get my way all the time, either. It means we're partners. Fifty-fifty."

"Agreed," he stated emphatically.

Chuckling, she squeezed his hands.

"So does this mean what I think it does?" he asked.

She took a deep breath. "I love you, John. And you're right. It's time I wasn't down. It's time I got up."

He bent and kissed her long and passionately until she felt it down to her toes. When they broke apart, she felt dazed. "And one more thing," she said.

He narrowed his eyes. "Yes?"

"The Buttucci brothers will always have a job with us as long as they want one." She gave him a look. "Even Biggie."

He sighed. "Agreed. But if he hurts my mother, I have the right to kick his butt."

"Agreed."

They kissed once more. She felt joy, relief and excitement all rolled into one. Slipping her arms around his waist, she hugged him close. "Oh, and I don't like long engagements, either"

She could feel him kiss the top of her head. "Agreed."

* * * * *

*Turn the page for a sneak peek at
Beckett and Andie's romance
coming next from author Syndi Powell...*

"Boss, we've got a problem."

Beckett paused at the words, resting the sledgehammer he'd been using to tear up the kitchen's ceramic tile floor. "Rob, I hired you so that we wouldn't have problems. What's wrong?"

The younger man shook his head. "I think you need to see this."

Beckett followed him into the living room of the house they'd started to renovate that morning. Rob pointed at the east living room wall. "There's two walls."

"Two?" He approached the wall and peered into the foot-wide hole where Rob had started to take down the drywall. Reaching for his cell phone from his back pocket, Beckett used the flashlight feature to try to examine what lay behind the outer wall.

Rob was right. There was a second wall behind the first. Why in the world would someone lose square footage by building it six inches out from the original wall?

Beckett turned back to Rob. "That explains why the room dimensions were off from the blueprints."

"What are we going to do about it?"

"Nothing. For now." He wanted time to think about it first before they acted rashly. "Why don't you tackle the master bedroom walls for now. We'll revisit this wall later."

Rob gave a nod and left Beckett who returned to the kitchen. He wanted to get this floor up before quitting for the day. He raised the sledgehammer over his head and brought it down on the ceramic. It felt good to break apart the tiles, straining his muscles as he hefted the hammer above his head again and again to smash it onto the floor. He found the demolition oddly satisfying when work on a house began. Later, he hoped he would find the same appreciation when he handed the keys over to the new owner and deposited their check into his bank account. But for now, he'd revel in the burn in his biceps as he smashed the hammer back down on to the tiles.

After an hour, he stopped to wipe his

forehead for the umpteenth time with an old bandanna he kept in the back pocket of his jeans. Rob popped his head into the room. "I'm taking off for the night and thought I'd join some buddies at the pub to celebrate the New Year. You in?"

Beckett put his bandanna back into his pocket, hoping it looked as if he was seriously considering the invitation, though he already knew his answer. After a moment, he shook his head. "I want to finish tearing up this floor tonight, then prime it for the new tiles."

Rob glanced at his watch. "It's already after seven. You planning on working all night?"

If he could, he would keep working on the house for days without sleeping. Because working made him stop thinking and kept him awake. Whereas sleeping only brought back the bad dreams. He gave Rob a shrug. "You go on. I'll see you bright and early tomorrow morning."

"Tomorrow is New Year's Day, and you gave me the day off." Rob frowned at him. "Are you okay, man?"

Beckett waved off his concern. "I'm fine.

I just forgot what day it was. I'll see you after the holiday."

Rob peered at him briefly and then nodded. "Maybe you could use a night out with the guys. Come with us, Beckett. I'll even buy the first round of beers."

The thought of sitting in a bar with people all around him made his heart stutter, and he swallowed at the bile that rose in his throat. "Another time."

"I'm holding you to that."

Beckett agreed, but acknowledged that it would never happen. He didn't go to loud public places like bars or restaurants. He'd put off Rob's invitations until the guy gave up on trying to include him. Beckett didn't see the need to be a part of the group anymore because he was better off on his own.

He returned to scooping up the tiles with a dust pan and tossing them into an empty cardboard box that he had repurposed earlier. He needed to work. To stay busy. To keep his mind occupied and away from thoughts of the past.

His stomach growled as he finished removing the last tile. Glancing at his watch, he realized it was almost nine, and he'd eaten lunch more than eight hours ago. No wonder his belly felt as if it was gnawing on itself. He left the house to walk to his truck parked in the driveway, pulled out the cooler he kept stocked with food for times such as this, and pulled out a salami sandwich. He returned to the warmth of the house and took a seat on an overturned bucket. Unwrapping the sandwich, he took a large bite and glanced around the living room as he ate. The wall behind the wall bothered him. What if the second wall hid a structural issue? While his inspector had assured him that the house was sound, it could be hiding a surprise.

He put his half-eaten sandwich down on the bucket and retrieved his sledgehammer from the kitchen. He swung the hammer into the wall, letting pieces of plaster fall on to the wooden floor. He pulled off a piece of the wall and tossed it aside, then hefted the sledgehammer over his shoulder, bringing it down on the next section of the wall. After thirty minutes, he'd opened up most of the first wall.

The rest was solid. He'd need his saw to remove the framing. What could all this effort be concealing? Excitement of the discovery pushed him to keep going.

With the framing now gone, he started to take down the inner wall even though his muscles protested at their continued use. But he couldn't stop now. He was desperate to find out what secrets the house was concealing from him.

Once he'd gotten the wall down to the studs, he paused and stared at the stained-glass window that had been revealed. He put a hand against the cool glass and wondered why anyone would ever cover up something so beautiful. They'd even bricked it over on the exterior side of the house. True, the cracks in the glass gave it an eerie beauty, but it looked amazing all the same. The window measured at least two feet across and four feet high, portraying a boat sailing by a lighthouse that sent out shards of light. Red and black glass bordered the window.

He took a step back. He didn't know anything about repairing windows much less stained glass. He fished his cell phone from a pocket and dialed up another friend in the contracting business. The call went to voicemail, so he waited for the beep. "Hey,

Cassie. Beckett here. I just found a stained-glass window in this house I'm flipping. Do you know anyone who might be able to fix it? I'd hate to tear it out and throw it in the trash. Call me."

He hung up the phone and returned to his sandwich. Sitting again on the bucket, he stared at the window and wondered what it all meant.

I promise I'm going to find out.

For more wonderful heartfelt romances from author Syndi Powell, please visit www.Harlequin.com today!

Get 4 FREE REWARDS!

We'll send you 2 FREE Books plus 2 FREE Mystery Gifts.

Love Inspired® books feature contemporary inspirational romances with Christian characters facing the challenges of life and love.

FREE Value Over **$20**

THE FORTUNES OF TEXAS COLLECTION!

18 FREE BOOKS in all!

Treat yourself to the rich legacy of the Fortune and Mendoza clans in this remarkable 50-book collection. This collection is packed with cowboys, tycoons and Texas-sized romances!